Praise for Erich Kästner

On *The Parent Trap* and *The Flying Classroom*

'There are so many books where it's the combination of author and illustrator that makes you love them. In the case of *The Flying Classroom* and *The Parent Trap*... it's the combo of author, illustrator and translator. The bold line drawings by Walter Trier are the work of genius... As for the stories, if you're a fan of *Emil and the Detectives*, then you'll find these just as spirited'

Melanie McDonagh, *Spectator* Children's Books of the Year

'A treasure-trove of childhood reading'

Huffington Post

'I enjoyed every word... before reluctantly passing them on to my grandson. They explore childhood with wit and invention while spinning magical yarns interwoven with the erratic and bizarre actions of adults and the independent-mindedness of children'

Amanda Hopkinson, *PEN Atlas* Books of the Year

'A perfect story for Christmas!... *The Flying Classroom* tells of the friendships and adventures of a group of lively boys... As Christmas gets ever closer, hopes and fears are raised and, in the final pages, beautifully resolved'

Julia Eccleshare, *Lovereading4kids* Children's Books of the Year

Dot & ANTON

ERICH KÄSTNER

Translated by Anthea Bell • Illustrated by Walter Trier

PUSHKIN CHILDREN'S BOOKS

Pushkin Children's Books

71–75 Shelton Street, London WC2H 9JQ

Dot and Anton was first published in German as *Pünktchen und Anton* in 1931 by Williams & Co. Verlag, Berlin

Text and illustrations © 1935 Atrium Verlag AG, Zürich

English language translation © Anthea Bell 2015

This translation first published by Pushkin Press in 2015

9 8 7 6 5 4

The translation of this work was supported by a grant from the Goethe-Institut which is funded by the German Ministry of Foreign Affairs

ISBN 978 1 782690 57 3

Set in Berling Nova by Tetragon, London

Proudly printed and bound in Great Britain by TJ International, Padstow, Cornwall on Munken Pure 120gsm

www.pushkinchildrens.com

Contents

This Introduction
is as Short as Possible

*W*hat was I going to say just now? Oh yes, I remember. The story that I'm about to tell you this time is extremely odd. It is odd because first, well, it just is odd, and second it really happened. It was in the newspaper about six months ago. Aha, you're thinking as you whistle through your teeth, Kästner's stolen someone else's story! But he hasn't.

The story in the newspaper was twenty lines long at the most. Not many people will have read it, because it was so short, only a little report saying that on such and such a day this, that and the other happened in Berlin. I went to find a pair of scissors at once, cut the report out of the newspaper and put it carefully away in the little box I keep for oddities. Ruth made me the little box for oddities out of cardboard and glue. It has a railway train with bright red wheels on the lid, and there are two dark green trees beside the train, and three white clouds as round as snowballs hovering overhead, all cut out of real shiny paper, lovely. The few other grown-ups who may have read the story too will hardly have noticed it. So far as they were concerned, the note in the newspaper will have been made of wood. What do I mean, wood? I mean it like this:

If a little boy fishes a piece of wood out from under the stove, and says to the wood, 'Gee up!', the wood turns into a horse, a real live horse. And if his big brother looks at the wood, shaking his head, and tells the little boy, 'That's not a horse at all, but you're certainly a donkey,' it makes no difference. It was much the same with my little story out of the newspaper. Other people thought: that's just a newspaper story twenty lines long. But I murmured, 'Abracadabra!' and it turned into a book.

I'm telling you this for a very specific reason. If you write stories, you very often get asked, 'Hey, you—did what you wrote really happen?' Children in particular always want to know that. And there you stand, with your big, fat head, tugging your little pointy beard. Because of course a lot of what's in your stories did really happen, but all of it? You don't go following people around the whole time with your notebook, writing down exactly what they said and did! Or then again, when something happened to them, you may not have known yet that you'd ever write about it. That's clear enough, isn't it?

But imagine a whole crowd of readers both large and small, planting themselves four-square in front of you and saying, 'My dear sir, if what you wrote didn't happen, it leaves us cold.' Then I'd like to say: it doesn't matter whether it really happened or not. What matters is for the story to be true! A story is true when it really could have happened just the way the writer told it. Did you understand that? Because if you did, then you've grasped an important rule of art. And if you didn't, never mind. And that, thank goodness, is the end of the introduction.

However, I know from experience that many children like reading things such as what I said just now about the piece of wood *and the horse, reality and truth. Other children would rather eat nothing but porridge for three days on end than put their minds to such difficult subjects. They're afraid their poor little brains might get creased. So what are we to do?*

I know a way out of that. I'll put everything to do with thinking in this book into small sections, I will call them 'afterthoughts', and I will ask the man who prints the book to make those ideas of mine look different from the story itself. I'll get him to print them in italics—that's lettering that slopes forward, like this introduction. So if you see something printed in italics, you can skip it if you like, as if it wasn't there at all. Do you understand? I hope you do, and I hope you're nodding your heads.

What was I going to say just now? Oh yes, I remember. I was going to say: and now the story can begin.

Chapter One

Dot Puts on a Show

W hen Mr Pogge got home at lunchtime he stood rooted to the spot, staring in surprise at the scene in the living room. There stood his daughter Dot with her face to the wall, bobbing little curtseys all the time and whimpering. I wonder whether she has a stomach ache, he thought. But he held his breath and stayed put. Dot reached both arms out to the silver-patterned wallpaper, bobbed a curtsey and said in a trembling voice, 'Matches, please buy my matches, ladies and gentlemen!' Piefke, Dot's little brown dachshund, was sitting beside her, looking puzzled and thumping his tail on the floor in time with her sales talk. 'Take pity on us poor people!' Dot went on pathetically. 'Only ten pfennigs a box.' Piefke the dog began scratching behind his ear. He probably thought the matches were too expensive, or maybe he was sorry he didn't have any money on him.

Dot raised her arms even higher, curtseyed and said, in faltering tones, 'My mother is totally blind, and still so young. Three boxes for twenty-five pfennigs. God bless you, kind lady!' Apparently the wall had bought three boxes of matches from her.

Mr Pogge laughed out loud. He'd never seen anything like it before. There stood his daughter in the living room, where the furniture and fittings had cost all of 3,000 marks, begging from the wallpaper. When she heard someone laughing Dot jumped, turned round, saw her father and ran out of the room. Piefke scurried unsympathetically after her.

'Have you gone soft in the head?' asked her father, but there was no reply. He turned and went into the study. There were letters and newspapers all over his desk. He sat down in his deep leather chair, lit a cigar and began reading.

Dot's real name was Luise. But she hadn't wanted to do much growing in her first few years of life, so they called her little Dot, and the nickname Dot stuck, although she had been going to school for a long time and wasn't so tiny any more. Her father, Mr Pogge, was the director of a walking-stick factory. He made a lot of money and had a great deal to do. However, his wife, Dot's mother, didn't agree. She thought he didn't make nearly enough money and worked much too hard. When she told him so, he always said, 'Women don't understand these things.' But she didn't really believe that.

They lived in a large apartment not far from the bank of the river where the Reichstag parliament building stood in Berlin. The apartment had ten rooms, and it was so large that when Dot got back to her own room after lunch she was usually feeling hungry again, after going all that way.

And speaking of lunch: Mr Pogge was hungry himself. He

rang the bell and Berta, the fat maid, came in. 'Am I going to starve?' he asked crossly.

'Oh no, sir!' said Berta. 'But madam is still out in town, and I thought...'

'Any more thinking and you won't get your day off tomorrow,' he said. 'Off you go—lunch! And call the governess and the child.'

Fat Berta set off at a trot, hurrying through the door like a ball rolling along.

Mr Pogge was first in the dining room. He took a tablet, made a face and drank some water to wash the tablet down. He took tablets whenever he had the chance. Before meals, after meals, before going to bed, after getting up. Some of the tablets were circular, some of them were rectangular, some of them were like little globes. You might have thought he took tablets for fun, but it was because he had stomach trouble.

Then Miss Andacht turned up. Miss Andacht was the governess. She was very tall, very thin and very crazy. 'She must have been dropped on her head as a baby,' fat Berta always used to say. Apart from that the two of them got on well. Earlier, when the Pogges didn't have a governess for Dot yet, and the nanny Käte was still there, Dot always liked sitting in the kitchen with Berta and Käte. They used to pod peas together, and Berta took Dot shopping with her and told her about her brother in America. And Dot had always been well and cheerful and didn't look as pale as she did these days, now that crazy Miss Andacht had joined the household.

'My daughter looks pale,' said Mr Pogge, sounding worried. 'Don't you think so too?'

'No,' said Miss Andacht. Then Berta brought in the soup and laughed. Miss Andacht squinted at the maid.

'Why are you laughing in that silly way?' asked the master of the house, spooning up soup as if he were being paid for it. But suddenly he dropped his spoon in the middle of his soup, put his napkin to his mouth, swallowed the wrong way, had a coughing fit and pointed to the door.

Dot was standing in the doorway. But goodness gracious, what did she think she looked like?

She had put on her father's red morning jacket and stuffed a pillow under it, so that she resembled a dented round teapot. Her thin bare legs, showing under the jacket, looked like drumsticks. Berta's Sunday hat perched unsteadily on her head. It was made of brightly coloured straw. Dot was holding the rolling pin and an open umbrella in one hand, and a piece of string in the other. A frying pan was tied to the string, and in the frying pan, which clattered over the floor behind Dot, sat Piefke the dachshund, frowning. He wasn't frowning because he was cross but because he had too much skin on his head. And as the skin didn't know where to go, it fell into folds.

Dot walked once round the table, stopped in front of her father, looked at him hard and said, 'May I see your tickets, please?'

'No,' said her father. 'Don't you recognize me? I'm the Minister of Railways.'

'Oh, I see,' she said.

Miss Andacht stood up, took Dot by the collar and removed all the extra clothes and other things until she looked like a normal child again. Fat Berta took the fancy dress outfit and the rolling pin and the umbrella out of the room. She was still laughing in the kitchen. You could hear her distinctly.

'How was school?' asked Dot's father, and as she didn't answer but just stirred the soup in her soup plate around, he went on, 'What's three times eight?'

'Three times eight? Three times eight is a hundred and twenty divided by five,' she said. Nothing much could surprise Mr Pogge the walking-stick factory director now. He worked out the sum in his head, and since it was right he went on with his lunch. Piefke had climbed up on an empty chair, propped his forepaws on the table, and seemed to be frowning as he made sure that they all finished their soup. He looked as if he were about to make a speech. Berta brought in the next course, chicken with rice, and gave Piefke a little slap. The dachshund misunderstood it, and got right up on the table. Dot put him down on the floor again and said, 'I wish I had a twin.'

Her father shrugged his shoulders regretfully.

'It would be great,' said Dot. 'We'd both wear the same clothes, and we'd have hair the same colour and take the same size of shoes, and we'd be just like each other and have the very same face.'

'So?' said Miss Andacht.

Dot groaned with delight when she imagined being one of twins. 'No one would know which was me and which was her. And if they thought one of us was me it would be my twin. And if they thought it was her then it would be me. Oh, it would be brilliant.'

'It'd be unbearable,' said her father.

'And when the teacher said, "Luise!", I'd stand up and say, "No, I'm the other one." And then the teacher would say, "Sit down!" and call to the other one and shout, "Why don't you stand up, Luise?" and she would say, "But I'm Karoline." And after three days of that the teacher would get spasms and have to go away to a sanatorium on sick leave, and we'd have holidays.'

'Twins usually look very different from each other,' claimed Miss Andacht.

'Karoline and I don't,' Dot contradicted her. 'You've never seen two people look so alike. Not even the director could tell us apart.' By the director she meant her father.

'One of you is quite enough for me,' said the director, helping himself to more chicken.

'What do you have against Karoline?' asked Dot.

'Luise,' he said in a loud voice. When he said 'Luise' like that, it meant she must stop arguing or she'd be sorry. So Dot kept quiet, ate chicken and rice and secretly made faces at Piefke, who was sitting on the floor close to her, until he felt so uncomfortable that he shook himself and ran off to the kitchen.

When they were eating dessert (it was greengages), Mrs Pogge finally turned up. She was very pretty, but strictly between ourselves she was also unbearable. Berta the maid had once told a colleague of hers, 'Someone ought to slap my mistress with a wet cloth. She has such a nice, funny child and such a charming husband, but do you think she bothers about either of them? Not a bit of it. She spends all day driving round town, shopping, taking things back to the shops to be exchanged, going to tea parties and fashion shows. And in the evening her poor husband has to trail along after her. Watching six-day bicycle races, going to the theatre or the cinema, balls, there's always something going on. She hardly comes home at all any more. Well, that has its good side.'

So Mrs Pogge turned up, sat down and looked hurt. Really she should have been the one to apologize for being so late. Instead she sounded insulted because they had started lunch without her. Mr Pogge took some more tablets, rectangular tablets this time, made a face and washed them down with a drink of water.

'Don't forget we're going to Consul General Ohlerich's party this evening,' said his wife.

'No, I won't,' said Mr Pogge.

'This chicken is cold,' she said.

'Yes, it is,' said fat Berta.

'Does Dot have homework to do?' she asked.

'No, she doesn't,' said Miss Andacht.

'Child, you have a tooth loose!' she cried.

'Yes, I do,' said Dot.

Mr Pogge got up from the table. 'I hardly remember what an evening at home is like any more.'

'Why, we never set foot outside the door yesterday evening,' replied his wife.

'But the Brückmanns were here,' he said, 'and the Schramms and the Dietrichs, the place was full of guests.'

'Were we at home yesterday or were we not at home yesterday?' she asked challengingly, looking at him hard. Mr Pogge the director said nothing, to be on the safe side, and went into his study. Dot followed him and sat down in the big leather armchair with him; there was room for them both. 'Your tooth is loose, is it?' he asked. 'Does it hurt?'

'It's not too bad,' she said. 'I'll pull it out sometime. Maybe today.'

Then a car horn hooted outside the building. Dot went to the front door with her father. Mr Hollack, the chauffeur, saluted her and she saluted him back. She did it just the same as the chauffeur, putting one hand to the peak of her cap, even though she wasn't wearing a cap. Her father got in the car, it drove away and her father waved. Dot waved back.

When she wanted to go back inside the apartment building, Gottfried Klepperbein was standing outside the door. He was the son of the couple who were caretakers of the building, and he was a total lout.

'Hey,' he said, 'if you give me ten marks I won't tell on you. If you don't I'll tell your father.'

'Tell him what?' asked Dot innocently.

Gottfried Klepperbein barred her way threateningly. 'You know perfectly well what, so don't act so stupid, sweetie.'

Dot wanted to get indoors again, but he wouldn't let her by. So she stood beside him, put her hands behind her back and looked up at the sky in surprise, as if the Zeppelin airship were flying overhead, or she'd seen a maybug with skates on, or something like that.

Of course the boy looked up at the sky too, and then Dot shot past him like lightning, leaving Gottfried Klepperbein with nothing for his trouble, as they say.

ABOUT DUTY

We met rather a lot of people in the first chapter, didn't we? Let's see whether we can remember them all.

There's Mr Pogge the director; his lady wife; there's Dot, their daughter; thin Miss Andacht; fat Berta; Gottfried Klepperbein; and Piefke the little dachshund. That's to say, we'll have to leave Piefke out. Dachshunds aren't really people, more's the pity.

And now I'll ask you the following question: which of those characters did you like, and which didn't you like so much?

If I may tell you my own opinion, I like Dot a great deal, and fat Berta too. I haven't made up my mind about Mr Pogge yet. But I can't stand Dot's mother.

There's something about the woman that bothers me. She doesn't look after her husband, so why did she marry him? She doesn't look after her child, so why did she have a baby? She's neglecting her duty, don't you agree? No one will mind her liking to go to the theatre or the cinema, or even watching six-day bicycle races for all I care. But first and foremost she's Dot's mother and Mr Pogge's wife.

And if she forgets that she can go take a running jump.

Can't she?

Chapter Two
Anton Can Even Cook

After lunch Mrs Pogge had a migraine. Migraines are headaches when you don't actually have a headache. Fat Berta had to let down the bedroom blinds so that it was all dark, like real night. Mrs Pogge lay down in bed and told Miss Andacht, 'Go for a walk with the child, and take the dog with you. I need peace and quiet. And I don't want anything to happen!'

Miss Andacht went to Dot's room to collect Dot and the dog. She arrived in the middle of a theatrical performance. Piefke was lying in Dot's bed, with only his nose showing. He was playing the part of the wolf who has eaten Little Red Riding Hood's grandmother. He didn't know the story, but he acted his part quite well. Dot was standing beside the bed wearing her red beret and with Berta's shopping basket over her arm. 'Oh, Grandmother,' she was saying, 'what big teeth you have!'

Then she switched to a different, deeper voice and growled, 'All the better to eat you with.' She put the basket down, went up to the bed and whispered to Piefke, like a prompter, 'Right, now you have to eat me.'

Piefke, as I said before, didn't know the story of Little Red

Riding Hood yet, so he turned over on his side and did nothing of the kind.

'Eat me!' Dot ordered him. 'Come on, eat me up this minute!' Then she stamped her foot and cried, 'Oh, for goodness' sake! Are you hard of hearing or what? You're supposed to be eating me!'

Piefke got cross, came out from under Dot's quilt, sat on the pillow and barked as loud as he could.

'He doesn't have a clue,' said Dot. 'He's a rotten actor.'

Miss Andacht put the clueless wolf's collar and lead on him, made sure that Dot was wearing her blue coat with the gilt buttons, and said, 'Get your linen hat. We're going for a walk.' Dot would really rather have kept her beret on, but Miss Andacht said, 'If you do that, then you can't go to see Anton.' The threat worked.

They left. Piefke sat down in the road so that Miss Andacht had to tug at his lead. 'He's going for a sleigh ride again,' said the governess, picking him up. He draped himself over her arm like a handbag that had been in an accident, darting her nasty looks.

'What street does Anton live in? Did you notice that?'

'Artilleriestrasse, fourth floor, on the right,' said Dot.

'What number is the building?'

'A hundred and eighty divided by five,' said Dot.

'Why don't you just say thirty-six and be done with it?'

'It's easier to remember my way,' claimed Dot. 'And incidentally, I think Berta smells a rat. She says someone must be positively devouring matches, she keeps buying more and they always go missing. I hope she won't find us out. And

Klepperbein's been threatening me again. He says he wants ten marks or he'll give us away. Suppose he tells the director, then what?'

Miss Andacht didn't reply. For one thing she wasn't naturally talkative, and for another she didn't like this conversation. They walked along beside the River Spree, crossed a small iron bridge, went up the Schiffbauerdamm, turned left down Friedrichstrasse, right at the corner, and then they were in Artilleriestrasse.

'It's a very old, ugly building,' remarked the governess. 'Watch out; there could be trapdoors in it.'

Dot laughed, picked Piefke up and asked, 'Where shall we meet later?'

'You can pick me up from the Café Sommerlatte at six.'

'Are you going dancing with your fiancé again? Give him my regards, and have a nice time!' Then their ways parted. Miss Andacht went off to go dancing, and Dot went into the strange apartment building. Piefke howled. He didn't seem to like the place.

Anton lived on the fourth floor. 'It's great that you've come to see me,' he said. After they had said hello they stood in the doorway for quite some time. The boy was wearing a large blue apron.

'This is Piefke,' Dot explained.

'Pleased to meet you,' said Anton, patting the little dachshund. And once again they stood there saying nothing.

'Go on, then, invite me into the sitting room,' Dot said at last.

Then they laughed, and Anton went ahead. He took Dot into the kitchen. 'I'm just cooking,' he said.

'You can cook?' she asked. Her jaw dropped, and stayed like that.

'Well, yes,' he said. 'What else are we to do? My mother's been ill for such a long time, so I do the cooking when I get back from school. We can't go hungry, can we?'

'Please don't let me disturb you,' said Dot. She put Piefke down, removed her coat and took her hat off. 'Go on cooking, and I'll watch. What are you cooking today?'

'Boiled potatoes with salt,' he said, picking up an oven cloth and going over to the stove. There was a pan standing on it. Anton took the lid off the pan, stuck a fork into the potatoes and nodded, satisfied. 'But she's much better now,' he said.

'Who is?' asked Dot.

'My mother. She said she'll get up for a couple of hours tomorrow. And she may go back to work next week. She works as a cleaning lady, you see.'

'Yes, I see,' agreed Dot. 'My mother doesn't work at anything. At the moment she has a migraine.'

Anton took two eggs, broke them into a pan, tipped the last of the eggs out of their shells and then threw the shells away in the coal scuttle, poured some water into the pan, put something white into it on top of the eggs and the water, and then took a little whisk and stirred the mixture up with it. 'Oh no!' he cried. 'It's going lumpy.'

Piefke trotted over to the coal scuttle and visited the eggshells.

'Why did you put sugar in that pan?' asked Dot.

'It was flour,' Anton told her. 'I'm making scrambled eggs, and if you add flour and water to the eggs you get bigger helpings.'

Dot nodded. 'How much salt do you add to the boiled potatoes?' she asked. 'A whole pound of salt or only half a pound?'

Anton laughed out loud. 'Much, much less than that!' he said. 'We want them to taste nice. Only enough salt to cover the tips of two knives, of course.'

'Of course,' said Dot, watching him. He took a small saucepan, melted some margarine in it and put it over the second gas flame, then he tipped the whisked eggs into it. They hissed. 'Don't forget the salt, Anton,' he reminded himself, taking a pinch of salt and sprinkling it over the yellow mixture in the small saucepan. When it began thickening he stirred it with a wooden spoon. There was an appetizing sizzle.

'So it's called scrambled eggs because they're all scrambled up,' Dot worked out.

'You go on stirring it for a bit, please,' asked Anton, handing her the spoon, and she stirred the mixture for him. He took hold of the handles of the pan of potatoes with two woollen cloths and tipped the simmering water down the sink. Then he divided the potatoes between two plates. 'You have to be terribly careful with boiled potatoes or they go all mushy,' he said.

But Dot wasn't listening. She was stirring the eggs so hard that her arm hurt. Meanwhile, Piefke was playing football with the eggshells.

Anton turned the gas off, divided the scrambled eggs fairly

between the two plates, washed his hands and took off the big apron.

'We couldn't come yesterday evening,' said Dot. 'My parents had guests, so they stayed at home.'

'That's what I thought,' said the boy. 'Just a moment. I'll be right back.'

He took the two plates and pushed his way through the door. Dot was left alone. She tried balancing an eggshell on Piefke's head. 'If you learn to do that,' she whispered, 'you can perform in the circus.' But the dachshund seemed to have some kind of objection to the circus. He kept throwing the eggshells off his head again. 'All right then, don't, you silly dog,' said Dot, looking round. Goodness, what a tiny kitchen this was! She had seen at once that Anton was a poor boy, but she was astonished to find that he had such a minute kitchen. You looked down from the window into a grey yard. 'What do you think of our kitchen by comparison?' she asked the dachshund. Piefke wagged his tail.

Then Anton came back. 'Would you two like to come into the bedroom while we eat?' he asked. Dot nodded, and took Piefke by the scruff of his neck.

'She still looks rather ill,' said the boy, 'but do me a favour and don't seem to notice, all right?'

It was a good thing that he had prepared Dot in advance. Anton's mother was sitting up in bed, looking very pale and unwell. She gave Dot a friendly nod and said, 'How nice of you to come to visit.'

Dot bobbed a curtsey and said, 'Enjoy your meal, Mrs Anton. You're looking very well. How is your esteemed health today?'

The boy laughed, put another pillow behind his mother's back and said, 'My mother's name isn't Anton. Anton is me.'

'Honestly, men!' said Dot, exasperated, rolling her eyes. 'What a lot of trouble they are, don't you agree, dear madam?'

'I'm not the sort you have to call madam,' explained Anton's mother, smiling. 'I'm Mrs Gast.'

'Gast,' repeated Dot. 'That's right, it says so on your door. It's a pretty name, too.' She had made up her mind to like everything she saw here, so as not to hurt the feelings of Anton and his mother.

'Does it taste all right, Mama?' he asked.

'It's delicious, my boy,' replied the sick woman, and she ate heartily. 'I'll be able to cook again myself tomorrow. You aren't getting any time to play, my dear, and your school work is suffering as well. Do you know, he even cooked ground-beef patties yesterday?' she told the girl. And Anton bent over his plate so as not to show how pleased he was by the praise.

'I don't understand the first thing about cooking,' Dot admitted. 'Fat Berta does it for us at home; she weighs a hundred and eighty pounds. But I can play tennis.'

'And her father has a car and a chauffeur,' said Anton.

'We'll take you for a drive in it if you like,' Dot told him. 'The director is a nice man. The director's my father,' she added.

'It's a big Mercedes, a real limousine,' Anton explained. 'And their apartment has ten rooms, too.'

'But yours is a lovely apartment as well, Mrs Gast,' said the girl, putting Piefke on the bed.

'How do you two come to know each other?' asked Mrs Gast.

Anton trod on Dot's toes and said, 'Oh, well, we just said hello in the street one day. We liked each other at once.' Dot nodded in agreement. Then she glanced at the dachshund and said, 'Ladies and gentlemen, I think Piefke needs to go out.'

Mrs Gast said, 'You could all go for a little walk, couldn't you? I'll have a nap for an hour or so.' Anton took the plates into the kitchen and went to fetch his cap. When he came back into the bedroom, his mother said, 'Anton, you ought to get your hair cut.'

'Oh no!' he protested. 'All those little hairs fall down the back of my neck, and they tickle horribly.'

'Give me my purse. You're going to get your hair cut,' she ordered.

'All right, if you're so keen on it,' he said. 'But I have the money for it myself.' And when his mother looked at him in an odd way, he added, 'I've been helping to carry people's luggage at the railway station.' He kissed his mother on the cheek and told her to sleep well, not to get up, to keep warm, and so on.

'Anything you say, doctor,' said his mother, offering Dot her hand.

'Goodbye,' Dot said. 'But now we must go. Piefke can't wait any longer.'

The dachshund was sitting by the door, looking hard at the handle as if he were trying to hypnotize it. That made all three of them laugh, and then the children went happily out.

ABOUT PRIDE

I wonder what you think. Do you think it's all right for a boy to cook? Put on his mother's apron, peel potatoes, put them in a pan and add salt to the water, and goodness knows what else?

I was talking to Paul about that, and he said, 'Well, I wouldn't cook. I've got no intention of cooking.'

'Hmm,' I said, 'but suppose your mother was ill in bed, and the doctor had said she needed to eat well and at regular intervals, or she might die?…'

'Oh, all right,' said Paul hastily, 'then I suppose I'd cook, like your friend Anton. But if you ask me, I'd be ashamed of myself all the same. Cooking's not something that boys do.'

'If you'd been playing with a dolls' kitchen, that might be some reason to feel ashamed of yourself,' I said. 'But if you were cooking to make sure your sick mother had food at the right time, you could be proud of that. You could be even prouder of it than you are of doing a long jump of four metres…'

'Four metres twenty,' said Paul.

'There, you see,' I said, 'you're really rather proud of that!'

'I've been thinking about it,' said Paul after a while, 'and maybe I wouldn't be ashamed if someone caught me cooking. But I'd rather no one did. I think I'd bolt the kitchen door. And anyway my mother isn't ill. And if she was we'd get a cleaning lady to come, and she could cook for us!'

Paul is a fathead, don't you think?

Chapter Three
Shaving a Dog

Piefke stopped at the first lamp post they came to. When the children wanted to go on, he wouldn't. Dot had to drag him. 'He's going for a ride on a sleigh again,' she said.

'Let me try,' said Anton. 'We'll soon get him moving.' He took hold of the dog's lead, and pulled his handkerchief far enough out of his pocket for a white corner of it to show. Then he called, 'Piefke!'

The dachshund raised his head, looked at the white corner of the handkerchief with interest, and thought: that could be something to eat. So when Anton walked on he waddled hastily after him, watching the handkerchief all the time and snuffling.

'Terrific!' said Dot. 'A brilliant idea. I must remember that.'

'What did you think of our apartment?' he asked. 'Not very nice, is it?'

'It looks a bit dilapissipated,' she said.

'What?' he asked.

'Dilapissipated!' she said. 'Do you like that word? I made it up. I sometimes discover new words. Warmometer is another of them.'

'Warmometer instead of thermometer?' he said. 'So you didn't mean what you said badly?'

'Not a bit,' she said. 'Shall we play at laughing?' She didn't wait for his answer, but took his hand and murmured, 'Oh dear, oh dear, I don't feel at all like laughing, I feel so deeply, tragically sad and sorrowful.' Anton looked at her, baffled. She opened her eyes very wide and frowned. 'Oh dear, oh dear, I don't feel at all like laughing, I feel so deeply, tragically sad and sorrowful,' she repeated. Then she nudged him in the ribs and said, 'Your turn!'

Anton did as she wanted. 'Oh dear, oh dear,' he murmured. 'I don't feel at all like laughing, I feel so deeply, tragically sad and sorrowful.'

'Me too, oh, I feel so sad,' she murmured back. 'I don't feel at all like laughing, I feel so deeply, tragically sad and sorrowful.' And because they were looking at each other with such utterly miserable expressions, they started roaring with laughter.

'Oh dear, oh dear, I don't feel at all like laughing,' Anton began again, and they laughed more than ever. Finally they dared not look at each other any more. They laughed and chuckled, they couldn't stop, they could hardly get their breath back. People were stopping to look at them. Piefke sat down. Now they've gone right out of their tiny minds, the dachshund thought. Dot picked him up, and the children went on. But they were careful to look in different directions. Dot chuckled to herself a few more times, and then it was over.

'My goodness, that was strenuous,' said Anton. 'I'm totally laughed out.' He wiped the tears of laughter from his eyes. And then they had reached the barber's shop. It was a very small one, and you had to climb a few steps up to it.

'Hello, Mr Habekuss,' said Anton. 'I'm supposed to get my hair cut.'

'That's fine. Sit down, sonny,' said Mr Habekuss. 'And how's your mother?'

'Thanks for asking. She's getting better. But things aren't any better about paying.'

'Same as usual, then,' said Mr Habekuss. 'Twenty pfennigs deposit, the rest in instalments, short at the back, a little longer in front, I know. And how about the little lady?'

'I'm only the audience,' said Dot. 'Don't let me put you off.'

Mr Habekuss tied a large white cloth round Anton and snipped away with his scissors.

'Does it tickle yet?' asked Dot. She couldn't wait to find out. And since Anton didn't answer, but sat perfectly still, she thought of something else to do. She put Piefke on the other chair, tied her handkerchief round his neck and rubbed shaving foam on his nose. At first Piefke thought the shaving foam was whipped cream, but the white stuff didn't taste nice, so he put his tongue back in his mouth and shook his head.

Dot pretended to be shaving Piefke. She gradually shaved the foam off him with her forefinger, danced round him and talked to him just as she'd heard barbers talking.

'Oh yes, sir,' she told the dachshund, 'what terrible times these are! Is my forefinger sharp enough for you? Terrible times. Enough to make anyone... well, you know what I mean. Just imagine—turn your head the other way, please—just imagine, I

get home yesterday to find that my wife has had triplets, three celluloid dolls, every last one of them a girl. With red grass growing on their heads. Enough to send anyone crazy, don't you think? And when I come to open up the shop first thing this morning, here's the bailiff saying he has to take my mirrors away. Why, I ask him, do you want to ruin me? Sorry, he says, but the Finance Minister has sent me. You don't eat rhubarb, you see. Shave you against the way the hair grows, sir? By the way, what makes you so nice and brown? Oh, I see, you use a sunlamp. Well, half an hour later along came the minister himself. We agreed that I'd shave him for a week for free, ten times a day. Yes, he does have a very strong growth of beard. Would you like any eau de Cologne? I'm going away soon. The Zeppelin wants to take a seasick hairdresser on its flight to the North Pole to cut the polar bears' hair. I'll bring you back a polar bear's skin if you like. Powder, sir?'

Dot put some white powder on the dachshund's nose, and Piefke stared at himself in the mirror, horrified. Mr Habekuss forgot about cutting Anton's hair, and Anton shook with amusement. Dot, in deadly earnest, now began reading out what the posters in the shop said, for a change. Sometimes she got their words mixed up. 'Use Dralle's new hairstyling lotion, you get the best prices for original articles in my shop, if you're satisfied tell other people, ears also pierced here, if you're not satisfied tell me, no more bald patches, the latest fashion, open from eight to ten on Sunday, gentlemen are asked to get their hair cut on weekdays, corns disinfected before treatment, razor blades an unnecessary nuisance, mind you don't develop tartar on your teeth.' She read all this in a boring, sing-song tone of voice, as if she were reciting a poem. Piefke got tired of it, rolled himself up on the chair and had a nap.

'Isn't she priceless?' Anton asked Mr Habekuss.

'Thanks for nothing,' said the barber. 'Two days of this and I'd be seeing white mice.' Then he pulled himself together and snipped with his scissors. He wanted to finish cutting Anton's hair and get this girl out of his shop. He had weak nerves.

Then another customer came in, a fat man in a white butcher's apron.

'Just coming, Mr Bullrich,' said the barber. Anton looked intently in the mirror, so as not to miss anything. The master butcher nodded off as soon as he was sitting down. Dot placed herself in front of him.

'Dear Mr Bullrich,' she asked the fat man, 'can you sing?' The butcher woke up, twisted his fat, red sausage fingers awkwardly and shook his head.

'Oh, what a pity,' said Dot. 'Then the two of us could have sung four-part duets. Can you at least recite a poem? Is there anybody there, said the traveller? Or, I come from haunts of coot and hern, I make a sudden sally?'

Mr Bullrich shook his head again and squinted at the newspaper hanging on a hook, but he didn't dare reach for it.

'Now for the last question,' said Dot. 'Can you do a handstand?'

'No,' said Mr Bullrich firmly.

'No?' asked Dot, regretfully. 'Forgive me for saying so, but I've never met anyone with so little talent in all my life.' Then she turned her back on him and went over to Anton, who was chuckling to himself. 'That's grown-ups for you,' she told her friend. 'They expect us to be able to do everything, arithmetic and singing, going to bed in good time and turning somersaults, and they don't have the faintest idea how to do it themselves. By the way, I have a wobbly tooth, want to look?' She opened her mouth and pushed the little white tooth around with her tongue. It wobbled like mad.

'You ought to get it pulled out,' said Anton. 'Take a length of thread, tie it round the tooth in a loop, fix the other end to the door handle, run away from the door, and it'll come out. Boom, just like that!'

'You're so practical, Anton,' said Dot, clapping him appreciatively on the back. 'Black or white?'

'Black or white what?' he asked.

'Thread,' she said.

'White,' said Anton.

'Right, I'll sleep on it,' said Dot. 'Have you nearly finished, Mr Habekuss?'

'You bet I have,' said the barber. Then he turned and said to Mr Bullrich, 'What a handful she must be to bring up, don't you agree?'

Out in the street, Dot took Anton's hand and asked, 'Was it very bad?'

'Well, it was quite something,' he said. 'I'm not taking you with me another time.'

'Don't, then,' she said, letting go of his hand.

They had already reached the Weidendammer Bridge. Dot was talking to the dog, but she couldn't stand Anton's silence for long. 'What's actually the matter with your mother?' she asked.

'She had a growth inside her. Then they took her to hospital and cut it out. I went to see her every day. My goodness, she looked so bad then, terribly thin and yellow as a quince. And now she's been at home for two weeks, and she's much better. The nurses were very nice to me. I think they thought my mother was going to die.'

'What sort of a growth was it?' asked Dot. 'Like a plant in a pot with leaves and flowers and so on? Did she swallow it accidentally?'

'No, I'm sure she didn't,' he said. 'I'd be certain to know if she had. No, it just grew inside her.'

'A geranium or a holly tree or something?' asked Dot, curiously.

'No, no, anything growing inside you must be skin and flesh. And if they don't get it out of you, then you die.'

After a while Dot stopped walking, clasped her hands over her stomach and wailed, 'Anton, dear Anton, there's something pushing against me in here. Watch out, I have a growth inside me too. I'm sure it's a little fir tree growing in my tummy. I like fir trees so much.'

'No,' said Anton. 'You don't have anything growing in your tummy. Bats in the belfry, that's what you've got.'

THE THIRD AFTERTHOUGHT IS:

ABOUT IMAGINATION

I'm sure you'll have noticed by now that Dot is a rather imaginative girl. She curtseys to the wall and sells it matches, she puts on fancy dress and pulls her dachshund along after her in a frying pan, she puts him to bed and imagines he's the big bad wolf and is going to eat her up. She asks Mr Bullrich the master butcher to sing four-part duets with her. Finally, she even imagines having a growth inside her. She imagines things that don't exist at all, or are entirely different in reality from the way she pictures them.

I once read about a man who had a vivid imagination, and so he had very lifelike dreams. For instance, he once dreamt of jumping out of the window. Then he woke up, and he really was lying in the street! Now, fortunately, he's moved to a ground-floor apartment. But imagine if the poor man had lived five floors up! Then his imagination could have been deadly dangerous. Imagination is a wonderful thing, but you have to keep it under control.

Chapter Four
Some Differences of Opinion

Meanwhile, Miss Andacht and her fiancé were sitting in the Café Sommerlatte, and sometimes they danced together. Little apple trees made of cardboard and paper stood between the tables, all of them in blossom and looking like the real thing. But as well as the paper blossom, brightly coloured balloons and paper streamers hung from the cardboard branches. The café looked nice, and the band was playing catchy dance tunes. Because she was so tall and thin, Miss Andacht hadn't really thought she'd ever have a fiancé, but she'd had one for the last two weeks, all the same. If only he hadn't been so strict with her! He was always ordering her about, and if she didn't do as he said at once he gave her such a nasty look that her ears stood out with fright.

'Did you understand?' he asked, leaning well forward as his eyes flashed angrily.

'Do you really want to do that, Robert?' she asked anxiously. 'I have two hundred marks in the savings bank, and you're welcome to have them.'

'What, your pathetic little savings, you silly cow?' he said. Which shows you that he wasn't exactly a gallant gentleman. 'I must have that plan of the place by tomorrow.'

Miss Andacht nodded humbly. Then she whispered, 'Hush, here come the children.'

Dot and Anton came over to the table. 'This is Robert the Devil,' Dot told Anton, pointing to the fiancé.

'Oh, Dot!' cried Miss Andacht, horrified.

'Never mind!' said her fiancé, with a fake smile. 'Your little princess is just having fun. Oh, what a cute little dog!' he added, and tried to pat the dachshund. But Piefke opened his mouth, growled and looked as if he was going to bite Robert. Then the children had to sit down. Miss Andacht's fiancé was going to order them hot chocolate, but Anton said, 'No thank you, sir, don't go to any unnecessary expense on our account.'

The band was beginning to play again, so Miss Andacht danced with her Robert. The children stayed at the table.

'Shall we dance too?' asked Dot.

Anton turned the idea down flat. 'After all, I'm a boy,' he said. 'By the way, I don't like that Robert a bit.'

'Nor do I,' said Dot. 'He has a look in his eyes like sharpened pencils. Piefke doesn't like him either. Apart from that it's splentastic here.'

'Splentastic?' asked Anton. 'Oh, I see, it's another of your invented words.'

Dot nodded. 'Anton, there's someone else I don't like. He's our caretaker's son. He said if I don't give him ten marks he'll tell my father about us. His name is Gottfried Klepperbein.'

'Oh, I know him,' said Anton. 'He goes to the same school as me, one class higher up. You just wait, I'll sort him out.'

'Great!' cried Dot. 'Only he's bigger than you.'

'Who cares?' said the boy. 'I'll take him apart.'

All this time Miss Andacht and her fiancé were dancing. So were a lot of other people. Robert squinted angrily at the children and whispered, 'Get those kids out of my sight. We'll meet here again tomorrow afternoon. And what are you going to bring with you?'

'The plan,' said Miss Andacht. It sounded as if her voice had sprained its ankle.

Out in the street Miss Andacht said, 'You dreadful child! Fancy annoying my fiancé like that!'

Dot didn't reply. She just rolled her eyes to make Anton laugh.

Miss Andacht's feelings were injured. She walked ahead with Piefke, striding along as if she were being paid for it. Almost before they knew it, they had reached the building where the Pogges lived.

'So we meet again this evening,' said Dot. And Anton nodded. As they were standing there, Gottfried Klepperbein happened to come out of the front door and was going to walk past them.

'Wait a moment,' said Anton. 'There's something important I want to tell you.' Gottfried Klepperbein stopped.

'Go indoors,' Anton told Dot.

'Are you going to take him apart now?' asked Dot.

'This isn't women's business,' he said. Miss Andacht and Dot went into the building. In fact Dot stopped on the other side of the door and peeked through the glass pane in it, but Anton didn't know that.

'You listen to me,' he told Gottfried Klepperbein. 'If you pester that girl again you'll answer to me for it. She's under my protection, understand?'

'You and your posh girlfriend!' laughed Klepperbein. 'You're plain daft!' At that moment he got his face punched so hard on one side that he sat down on the pavement. 'Hey, hang on!' he shouted, jumping to his feet. But then he got his face punched again, this time on the other side, and he sat straight down again. 'Just you wait,' he said, but for safety's sake he stayed put.

Anton took a step closer. 'I told you so without any bad feeling today,' he said, 'but if I ever hear any more about it I'll get rough with you.' And, so saying, he walked past Gottfried Klepperbein and didn't give him another glance.

'Gadzooks!' said Dot, watching from inside the door. 'The things that boy can do!'

Miss Andacht was already in the apartment. As she passed the kitchen fat Berta, who was sitting on a kitchen chair peeling potatoes, called out, 'Come a little closer, will you?'

Miss Andacht didn't want to go closer one bit, but she did as she was told. She was afraid of Berta.

'Listen,' said Berta, 'my room is three flights of stairs higher up, in the attic storey. But all the same I can tell that something's not right here. Will you kindly tell me why that child has been looking so pale recently, and has such dark rings under her eyes? And why she won't get out of bed early in the morning?'

'Dot is growing,' said Miss Andacht. 'She needs cod-liver oil or an iron tonic.'

'You've been a pain in the neck for a long time,' said Berta. 'If I ever find out that you have secrets, you'll be the one drinking cod-liver oil, bottle and all!'

'You're much too common for me,' said the governess, with her nose in the air. 'Don't think you can insult me.'

'So I can't insult you?' asked fat Berta, getting to her feet. 'We'll see about that. You silly dope, you sneaky great beanpole, you stupid spook, you can go and drink coffee out of the gutter, you—'

Miss Andacht put her hands over her ears, narrowed her eyes in fury and stalked along the corridor like a giraffe.

THE FOURTH AFTERTHOUGHT IS:

ABOUT COURAGE

At this point I'd like to say a few things about courage. Anton has just punched a bigger boy's face twice, and you might think Anton was showing courage. However, it wasn't courage at all, it was rage. And there's a little difference, not just in their first few letters.

You can show courage only when you're doing something in cold blood. If a doctor injects himself with dangerous bacteria and then with an antidote that he's invented, because he wants to find out if he's right about it, he's showing courage. If a polar explorer drives a few dog sleighs to the North Pole to make discoveries, that's courage. If Professor Piccard goes up into the stratosphere in a balloon, although no one has ever gone as high as that before, then it's courage too.

Did you follow the news story about Professor Piccard? It was interesting. He tried taking the balloon up again and again, but then he kept putting it off because the weather wasn't suitable. The newspapers made fun of him. People laughed when they saw his photographs. But he was waiting for the right moment. He was so courageous that he'd rather have people laughing at him than do something stupid. He wasn't a daredevil, he wasn't crazy, he was simply courageous. He wanted to find something out, he didn't want to be famous.

You don't prove your courage just with your fists, your head has to come into it.

Chapter Five
Do-it-yourself Dentistry

Mr Pogge the director was still at his walking-stick factory. His lady wife was still lying in the bedroom, passing the time by having a migraine. Miss Andacht was sitting in her room.

Dot and Piefke were eating supper on their own. Dot went to get a reel of white thread from Berta, and told the dachshund, who was sitting in his basket feeling rather tired, 'Now, watch this, little one!'

Dot tore a length of thread off the reel, looped one end round the wobbly tooth and fastened it with a knot, then tied the other end to the door handle. 'Here goes,' said Dot. 'Brrr!' she added, shivering. Then she slowly walked away from the door until the thread was stretched tight. She moved a little way farther, groaned pitifully and made a desperate face. She walked back to the door, and the thread went loose again. 'Oh, Piefke, Piefke,' she said, 'I'll never make a dentist.' Then she walked away from the door once more, but she was already wailing before the thread was taut.

'It's no good,' she said. 'Maybe if Anton was here I might risk it.' She leant against the door and thought hard.

'Shake paws, Piefke,' she ordered. But Piefke couldn't do

that yet. Dot bent down, picked up the dachshund and lifted him onto her little desk. She tied the free end of the thread to Piefke's left hind leg. 'Now, jump down!' she told him.

Instead of jumping, Piefke curled up and was obviously thinking of having a nice long sleep on the desk.

'Jump down!' Dot muttered in threatening tones. Resigning herself to her fate, she closed her eyes.

The little dachshund pricked up his ears, as well as he could with such floppy ones. But he still wasn't going to jump.

Dot opened her eyes again. She'd gone through all that anxiety in advance for nothing. She shoved Piefke, and now there was nothing for it; he had to jump down to the floor. 'Has the tooth come out yet?' she asked him. The dog didn't know either. Dot felt the inside of her mouth. 'No,' she said. 'The thread's too long, dear boy.'

She climbed up on the stool that stood at the desk, with Piefke under her arm, and then bent down to put him on the desk again. 'If this doesn't work,' she muttered, 'I'll have myself given chloroform.' She gave Piefke a little push, he slid over the desk, Dot stood bolt upright. The dog sailed over the side of the desk and dropped to the floor.

'Ow!' screeched the child. She could taste blood. Piefke hopped into his basket. He was glad not to be tied to anything any more. Dot wiped a few tears out of her eyes. 'Oh, my word!' she said, looking for a handkerchief. At last she found one, put it in her mouth and bit down on it. The thread was hanging over the side of the dog's basket, and a small white tooth lay in the middle of the room. Dot freed Piefke from the thread, picked up the tooth and danced round the room. Then she rushed off to see Miss Andacht.

'My tooth's come out, my tooth's come out!' she cried.

Miss Andacht quickly covered up a piece of paper. She was holding a pencil in her right hand. 'Oh yes?' she said, and that was all.

'What's the matter with you?' asked Dot. 'You've been acting very strangely for the last few days. Haven't you noticed that yourself? What's up?' She stood beside the governess, took a surreptitious look at the piece of paper, and said, as if she were her own grandfather, 'Come on, then, pour your heart out!'

Miss Andacht didn't in the least want to pour her heart out. 'When does Berta have her day off?' she asked.

'Tomorrow,' said Dot. 'Why do you want to know?'

'I just wondered,' said the governess.

'You just wondered?' asked Dot indignantly. 'That's a fine kind of answer!'

But she couldn't get any more out of the governess that day. You'd have thought every word cost money. So Dot pretended to stumble, and brushed against Miss Andacht's arm. The piece of paper came into view. It was covered with rectangles drawn in pencil. The words 'Living Room' were written on one rectangle, and the word 'Study' on another. But the next moment the governess's large, dry hands were lying over it again.

Dot didn't know what to make of that. I must tell Anton this evening, she thought. Maybe he'll understand it.

An hour and a half later she was in bed. Miss Andacht was sitting beside her reading aloud the fairy tale of the hedgehog and his wife. There we are, thought Dot, the two hedgehogs look just like twins. I was right at lunchtime. If I were a twin, and the other twin was called Karoline, we could win any race in sports lessons.

Then her parents came into her room. Her mother was wearing a beautiful silk evening dress and a pair of golden shoes, and her father was in a dinner jacket. They both gave their daughter a goodnight kiss, and Mrs Pogge said, 'Sleep well, darling.'

'I will,' said Dot.

Her father sat down on the edge of her bed, but his wife said firmly, 'Come along, you know the Consul General likes punctuality.'

The little girl nodded to her father. 'Don't do anything stupid, Director!' she said.

No sooner had her parents left than Dot jumped out of bed and cried out, 'Let's go!' Miss Andacht hurried into her room, got a torn old dress out of the chest of drawers and took it to the child. She herself put on a patched skirt and a faded old sweater. 'Are you ready?' she asked.

'You bet!' said Dot happily, although she was a sorry sight in her torn dress. 'You haven't put your headscarf on yet,' she told the governess.

'Now where did I leave it the day before yesterday?' Miss Andacht asked, but then she found it, tied it over her head, put on a pair of glasses with blue-tinted lenses, brought a shopping bag out from under the sofa and, thus disguised, the two of them stole out of the house.

Ten minutes after they had left, Berta came quietly creeping down the stairs from her maid's room up in the attics, or at least as quietly as fat Berta could creep. She knocked gently on Dot's door, but there was no answer.

I wonder if the little shrimp's asleep yet, she asked herself. Maybe she's just pretending not to hear me. And I only wanted to give her a piece of the cake I baked today, but since that minx Miss Andacht has been here I daren't go into Dot's room any more. When I opened the door the other day I nearly collided with my fine lady. The sleep before midnight is the best, says she, and mustn't be disturbed. Sleep before midnight, what nonsense! Nowadays Dot sometimes looks as if she didn't get a wink of sleep all night. And all that fuss and to-do and whispering. Well, I don't know, but things seem to me rather peculiar here just now. If it weren't for the director and Dot, I'd have given notice long ago.

'Don't you dare,' she threatened Piefke, who was sitting up in his basket outside Dot's door and snapping at the piece of cake. 'Lie down, Piefke, and let's not have a squeak out of you. Here, you can have a little bit, but then keep quiet. You're the only one in this household who isn't keeping secrets from me.'

ABOUT CURIOSITY

When my mother reads a novel she does it like this: she reads the first twenty pages and then the end, then she skims the parts in between, and then she really starts reading the book all the way through. Why does she do that? Before she can read the story in peace she has to know how it will end. Otherwise it gives her no rest at all. Mind you don't get used to that kind of thing! And if you happen to be doing it already, then wean yourselves off it, okay?

Because it's as if you went rummaging round in your mother's wardrobe two weeks before Christmas, so as to find out in advance what your presents will be. And when it comes to the present-giving, you'll already know about it. Don't you think that's terrible? You'll have to pretend to be surprised, but you'll have known what your presents are for ages, and your parents will wonder why you're not really delighted. Their Christmas will be spoilt, and so will yours.

And even when you were searching the wardrobe and found the presents two weeks early, you wouldn't have really been enjoying yourselves for fear of being taken by surprise. You just have to know how to wait. Curiosity is the death of delight.

Chapter Six
The Children on
the Night Shift

D o you know the Weidendammer Bridge? Have you ever
seen it in the evening, when the neon advertisements are
shining there under the night sky? Display boxes cover the
façades of the Comic Opera House and the Admiral's Palace
Theatre, and the ads are picked out in fluorescent writing
inside them. At the gable end of another building, on the
other side of the River Spree, there's an advertisement for a
well-known brand of washing powder shown by a thousand
flickering electric light bulbs; you see a huge cauldron with
steam coming from it, a snow-white shirt rises in the steam
like a friendly ghost, and then there's a whole series of coloured pictures. And beyond, above the buildings along the
Schiffbauerdamm, you see the gable end of the Grand Theatre
shining brightly.

Columns of buses roll over the arch of the bridge, with
Friedrichstrasse Station rising in the background. Elevated
railway lines run over the city from that station. The train
windows are brightly lit, and the carriages wind their way into

the night like shimmering snakes. Sometimes the sky looks pink with the reflection of all the lights shining down below.

Berlin is a beautiful city, particularly seen from this bridge, and most of all in the evening. Friedrichstrasse itself is a street crowded with cars. The street lights shine, car headlights flash, and throngs of people make their way along the pavements. The trains whistle, the buses clatter, the cars hoot their horns, the people talk and laugh. There's so much life going on there, children!

A poor woman, thin and wearing dark glasses, was standing on the bridge. She held a shopping bag and a few boxes of matches. Beside her, a little girl in a torn dress was bobbing curtseys to the passers-by. 'Matches, please buy my matches, ladies and gentlemen!' the little girl was pleading in a trembling voice. Many people walking along the bridge went straight past the two of them. 'Have a heart, please take pity on us poor people!' cried the child in pathetic tones. 'Only ten pfennigs a box!' A fat man coming towards them put his hand in his pocket.

'My mother is totally blind, and still so young,' stammered the girl. The fat man gave her a small coin and walked on. 'God bless you, kind lady!' said the child. The tall, thin woman dug her in the ribs. 'That wasn't a lady, it was a man, you silly thing,' muttered the woman crossly.

'Are you blind or aren't you?' asked the little girl, sounding injured. But then she bobbed another curtsey and asked, in her trembling voice, 'Matches, please buy our matches, ladies and gentlemen!' This time an old lady gave her a coin and a friendly nod.

'Business is booming,' the child whispered. 'We've already made two marks thirty, and we've only had to give five boxes of matches in return.' Raising her voice, she cried plaintively again, 'Have a heart, take pity on us poor people. Only ten pfennigs a box of matches!' Suddenly she hopped happily and waved. 'There's Anton on the other side of the street,' she told her companion. But then she hunched her shoulders again, bobbed curtseys and wailed hard enough to terrify the passers-by. 'Thank you, thank you kindly,' she cried. Their capital was growing. She threw the money she had been given into the shopping bag, where it fell on the other coins with a cheerful clink. 'Are you really going to give all that money to your fiancé?' she asked. 'Won't he just be pleased!'

'Hold your tongue,' the woman ordered.

'Well, it's true,' replied Dot. 'Why else are we standing here evening after evening hanging around like this?'

'Don't you say another word!' the woman muttered crossly.

'Matches for sale, buy my matches, ladies and gentlemen!' wailed Dot again, because more people were coming past. 'I'd rather we gave Anton some of it. He'll be standing on the wrong side of the road until Saturday.' Suddenly she squealed as if someone had kicked her. 'Here comes that nasty Klepperbein!'

Anton was indeed standing at the other side of the bridge, on the wrong side of the road running over it; not many people walked on that side. He was holding a small case open in front of him, and when anyone passed he said, 'Brown or black shoelaces for lace-up shoes? Or please buy some matches, they always come in useful.' He didn't have a very good line in sales talk or much of a gift for complaining, although he really did feel more like crying than laughing. He had promised the landlord to pay him five marks rent the day after next, and the housekeeping money had run out again. He needed to buy margarine tomorrow, and he was even planning to get a quarter-pound of liver sausage.

'You ought to be in bed, not here,' a gentleman told him.

Anton looked at him in surprise. 'But I like begging,' he murmured.

The man felt a little ashamed of himself. 'Well, never mind,' he said. 'Don't be cross.' And then he gave him a coin—a whole fifty pfennigs!

'Thank you very much,' said Anton, offering him two pairs of shoelaces.

'I'm wearing pull-on boots,' the gentleman explained as he took his hat off to the boy and hurried away.

Anton, feeling pleased, looked at his friend Dot on the other side of the bridge. Hello, wasn't that Klepperbein with her? He closed his case and hurried over the road. Gottfried Klepperbein had planted himself in front of Dot and Miss Andacht and was staring at them cheekily. Dot was putting out her tongue at the caretaker's son, but the governess was trembling in alarm. Anton kicked Klepperbein's backside. The boy swung round furiously, but when he saw Anton Gast standing there he remembered getting his face punched that afternoon and went off at a steady run.

'There, we're rid of him,' said Dot, giving Anton her hand.

'Come on,' said Miss Andacht. 'Let's go to the self-service café.'

'Good idea,' said Dot, taking Anton's hand and going ahead with him. Miss Andacht called her back. 'Aren't you going to guide me? What will people think if I set off just like that in spite of my dark glasses?' So Dot took the governess's hand and led her off the bridge, along Friedrichstrasse and towards the Oranienburger Gate underground station.

'How much have you made?' she asked Anton.

'Ninety-five pfennigs,' said the boy sadly. 'One gentleman gave me fifty pfennigs. Apart from that I might as well pack it in.'

Dot pressed something into his hand. 'Here, have this,' she whispered mysteriously.

'What's going on?' asked Miss Andacht in suspicious tones.

'Curiosity killed the cat,' said Dot. 'I don't ask you what those funny drawings of yours are, do I?'

Miss Andacht didn't say anything in reply to that. It was as if she had been struck by lightning.

The street was fairly empty here. The governess took off her dark glasses and let go of Dot's hand. They turned a couple of corners, and then they had reached their destination.

ABOUT POVERTY

About 150 years ago, the poorest people in the city of Paris went to Versailles, where the King of France and his wife lived. It was a demonstration. I'm sure you know what a demonstration is. The poor people stood outside the palace and called out, 'We have no bread to eat! We have no bread to eat!' They were very badly off.

Queen Marie Antoinette stood at the window and asked a high officer of state, 'What do the people want?'

'Your Majesty,' said the officer of state, 'they want bread. They don't have enough bread, and they are very hungry.'

The Queen shook her head in surprise. 'They don't have enough bread to eat?' she asked. 'Then let them eat cake!'

You may think that she was laughing at the poor people when she said that. But she didn't know what poverty means. She thought that if there didn't happen to be enough bread in the house, you could simply eat cake instead. She didn't know the people, she didn't know about poverty, and that was why her head was chopped off a year later.

Don't you agree that it would be easier to do away with poverty if only rich people had known, when they were children, what it was like to be poor? Don't you think that then the rich children would say: when we're grown up, and we own our fathers' banks and landed estates and factories, we'll make sure life is easier for workers—the workers who had been their childhood playmates?

Do you think that would be possible? Will you help to make sure that it is?

Chapter Seven
Miss Andacht Gets Tipsy

There were sometimes odd people standing or sitting around in the café, and Dot liked going to it because she thought it was so interesting. Sometimes there were even drunks there!

Anton yawned. He was so tired that his eyes were half closed. 'It was terrible,' he said, 'I dropped off to sleep in the arithmetic lesson today. Mr Bremser shouted at me so loud that I almost fell off the bench. He said I ought to be ashamed of myself, and my homework left much to be desired these days. And if it went on like this, he said, he was going to write a letter to my mother.'

'Oh, for heaven's sake,' said Dot. 'That's all we needed. Doesn't he know that your mother is ill, and you have to cook the meals and earn money?'

'How would he know that?' asked Anton curiously.

'From you, of course,' said Dot.

'I'd sooner bite my tongue off,' said Anton.

Dot didn't understand that. She shrugged her shoulders and turned to Miss Andacht, who was sitting in her corner staring straight ahead. 'I thought you'd invited us here,' she said.

Miss Andacht jumped, and slowly came back to her senses. 'What would you like?'

'Oranges with whipped cream,' suggested Dot, and Anton nodded. The governess stood up and went over to the buffet counter.

'Where did you get the money you gave me just now?' asked the boy.

'Miss Andacht only gives the money we make to her fiancé, so I kept some of it back. Hush, no arguing,' she said sternly. 'Watch out, I bet she'll be having cognac again. She drinks, poor soul. Listen, she was sitting in her room today drawing rectangles in pencil, and it said "Living room" on one of them and "Study" on another. That was all I saw.'

'It must have been the plan of an apartment,' said Anton.

Dot clapped her hand to her forehead. 'I'm an idiot,' she said. 'To think I didn't work that out for myself! But why would she be drawing plans of apartments?' Anton didn't know the answer to that either. Then Miss Andacht came back, bringing the children dishes of orange segments. She herself was drinking cognac. 'We must have made at least three marks,' she said. 'But there's only one mark eighty in my pocket. Can you understand it?'

'Maybe there's a hole in your pocket?' suggested Dot.

Miss Andacht investigated her pocket at once. 'No, there isn't,' she said.

'That's funny,' said Dot. 'You might almost think someone had stolen it.' Then she sighed, and said, 'What terrible times these are.'

Miss Andacht said nothing, drained her glass and went to get another cognac. 'First we stand about on the bridge for hours on end,' said Dot crossly, while Miss Andacht was buying her cognac, 'and then she drinks all the takings!'

'You'd better stay at home,' Anton told her. 'If your parents find out about this there'll be trouble.'

'Who cares?' said Dot. 'I didn't choose my governess, did I?'

Anton picked up a paper napkin lying on the next table, folded it to make a little bag and put six orange segments in it. Then he stowed the little bag away in his case. And when Dot looked at him inquiringly he said, sounding embarrassed, 'They're for my mother, that's all.'

'That reminds me of something,' she said, searching her little bag. 'Here!' She had something in her hand.

He bent over it. 'A tooth,' he remarked. 'Did your tooth come out, then?'

'What a silly question,' she said, sounding injured. 'Do you want it?'

The boy didn't really understand about teeth, so she put it back in her bag. Then Miss Andacht joined them again, obviously more than a little bit tipsy, and said it was time to leave. They walked to the Weidendammer Bridge together and said goodnight there.

'Is Mr Bremser your class teacher?' asked Dot.

Anton nodded.

'I'll come and see you again tomorrow afternoon,' she promised. Pleased, Anton shook hands with her, made Miss Andacht a bow, and hurried away.

Dot and Miss Andacht got home to the Pogges' apartment without any incidents. Dot's parents were still at Consul General Ohlerich's party. She went to bed and fell asleep at once. Piefke growled quietly because he'd been woken up. The governess went to her room, put her beggar woman's clothes away in her chest of drawers, and then she went to bed as well.

Anton couldn't go to bed yet. He stole quietly along the corridor, past his mother's room, put on a light in the kitchen, hid his little case, sat down at the kitchen table, propped his head in his hands and yawned so widely that he almost dislocated his jaw. Then he took a blue notebook and a pencil out of his pocket and opened the notebook. One page said 'Expenditure'. The opposite page was headed 'Earnings'. He reached into his trouser pocket, put a pile of small coins on the table and counted them with close attention. They came to two marks fifteen. If it hadn't been for Dot and the kind gentleman I'd only have forty-five pfennigs now, he thought, entering the evening's takings in his notebook under 'Earnings'.

With the money that he was secretly keeping in his paintbox, he had five marks sixty pfennigs, and the landlord wanted five marks just for the rent. They would be left with sixty pfennigs for food. He looked in the little larder. There were still some potatoes, and a piece of bacon rind lying on the chopping board. If he rubbed a pan well with the bacon rind tomorrow, perhaps they could have fried potatoes. But yet again his hopes of a quarter-pound of liver sausage would come to nothing, and he did like liver sausage so much. He took off his shoes, put the orange segments on a plate, switched off the light and stole out of the kitchen. He stopped at the bedroom door and laid his ear against the wood of it. His mother was asleep. He could hear her peaceful breathing, and sometimes she even snored slightly. Anton caressed the door, and smiled because just then she did give a little snore. Then he crept into the living room. He undressed in the dark, hung his suit over a chair, put the money in his paintbox, got on the sofa and covered himself up.

Had he closed the door to the corridor? Was the gas turned off? Anton tossed and turned restlessly, then he got up again and went to see whether everything was all right.

Yes, everything really was all right. He lay down once more. He had done his arithmetic homework. He had prepared for tomorrow's dictation in class. He hoped Mr Bremser wouldn't write his mother a letter, because then it would come out that he spent his evenings standing on the Weidendammer Bridge selling shoelaces. Did he still have enough shoelaces? The brown ones wouldn't last much longer. People seemed to wear brown shoes more often than black shoes. Or did brown shoelaces wear out more quickly?

Anton turned on the side where he slept best. He hoped his mother would get really better again. And then, at last, he fell asleep.

ABOUT THE FACT THAT LIFE IS SERIOUS

Not so long ago I was at the Christmas fair in Rostock in the north of Germany. The streets there go downhill to the River Warnow, they were lined with stalls, and down on the bank there were merry-go-rounds in full swing. Everything was so nice and noisy that I felt cheerful too, so I went over to a stall selling confectionery and asked for ten pfennigs' worth of Turkish honey in a little cardboard dish. It tasted delicious.

Then along came a boy with his mother. He was tugging at her sleeve and demanding, 'I want another packet of honey and ginger biscuits!' But I saw that he was already carrying five packets of those special Christmas cookies under his arm. His mother ignored him. So he stopped, stamped his foot and yelled, 'I want another packet of honey and ginger biscuits!'

'But you already have five packets,' his mother told him. 'Just think, poor children don't get any honey and ginger biscuits at all!'

What do you think the boy said then?

He lost his temper and shouted, 'Why should I bother about the poor children?' It startled me so much that I almost swallowed my Turkish honey and its little cardboard dish both at once. Good heavens, children, would you think it possible?

I mean, a boy like that hasn't earned the luck to have parents who are well off, and then he stands there shouting, 'Why should I bother about the poor children?' instead of giving two of his five packets of honey and ginger biscuits to poor children, and feeling glad that he can do something nice for them!

Life is serious, and life is difficult. And if the people who are well off don't, of their own free will, want to help those who aren't, then everything will come to a bad end.

Chapter Eight

Light Dawns on Mr Bremser

On Friday Dot left school an hour earlier than usual. Mr Pogge the director knew about that, and sent the chauffeur and the car to bring his daughter home. He didn't need the car himself at that time of day, and Dot loved going for a drive.

The chauffeur put his hand to the peak of his cap when she came out of the school gate and opened the car door for her. 'Hello, Mr Hollack,' she said. The other little girls were already looking forward to seeing him too, because when Dot Pogge was fetched from school by car, as many of them as would fit into it always came with her. But today Dot turned as she was getting in, looked at them all regretfully and said, 'I'm sorry, but if you don't mind I'm going on my own today.' Her friends' faces fell. 'There's something important that I have to do,' Dot explained, 'and you'd only be in my way.'

Then she sat down in the big car on her own, told the chauffeur an address, he got into the car himself and off they went, leaving twenty little girls sadly watching the beautiful car drive away.

A little later the car stopped outside a large building—and guess what, it was another school!

'Dear Mr Hollack,' said Dot, 'could you wait here for a moment, please?' Mr Hollack nodded, and Dot ran quickly up the steps. It was still break. She climbed to the first floor and asked a boy the way to the staffroom. He took her there, she knocked on the door, and since no one opened it she knocked again, quite hard this time.

The door opened, and she saw a tall young gentleman standing in front of her, eating a sandwich. 'Is that a nice sandwich?' Dot asked.

He laughed. 'And what else would you like to know?'

'I've come to speak to Mr Bremser,' she explained. 'My name is Pogge.'

The teacher finished his mouthful and then said, 'Right, come along in.' She followed him into a large room full of chairs. There was a teacher sitting on each of those many chairs, and that gruesome sight made Dot's heart beat faster. Her companion took her over to the window and a fat, bald-headed old teacher who was leaning against it. 'Bremser,' said Dot's escort, 'may I introduce Miss Pogge? She wants to speak to you.'

Then he left them alone.

'You want to speak to me?' asked Mr Bremser.

'That's right,' she said. 'You know Anton Gast, don't you?'

'He's in my class,' said Mr Bremser, looking out of the window.

'Exactly,' said Dot, satisfied. 'I see we understand each other.'

Mr Bremser was beginning to feel curious. 'What about Anton, then?'

'He went to sleep in the arithmetic lesson,' Dot told him. 'And I'm afraid you're not happy about his homework these days.'

Mr Bremser nodded, and said, 'That's correct.' By now some of the other teachers who wanted to hear what was going on had joined them.

'Excuse me, gentlemen,' Dot said, 'but please would you go back to where you were before? I have to speak to Mr Bremser privately.' The teachers laughed, and sat down on their chairs again. But they said hardly anything to each other, and kept their ears pricked.

'I'm Anton's friend,' Dot told Mr Bremser. 'He told me that if things went on like that you were going to write his mother a letter.'

'Yes, indeed. He even took out a notebook in the geography lesson just now and did sums in it. That letter will be going off to his mother today.'

Dot would have liked to find out whether she could see her reflection in Mr Bremser's shiny bald head, but there wasn't time for that now. 'Please listen hard,' she said. 'Anton's mother is very ill. She was in hospital, where they cut a plant out of her—no, it was a growth—and now she's been in bed at home for weeks and can't go to work.'

'I didn't know that,' said Mr Bremser.

'So she stays in bed and can't cook. But someone has to do the cooking! Do you know who does it? Anton does the cooking. I can tell you he cooks delicious things, boiled potatoes with scrambled egg and so on, it's great!'

'I didn't know that,' Mr Bremser repeated.

'His mother hasn't been able to earn any money for weeks, either. But someone has to earn money. And do you know who earns it? Anton earns money for them. Of course you didn't know that either.' Dot was losing her temper. 'Actually, what *do* you know?'

The other teachers laughed. Mr Bremser went red in the face and right over his bald head as well. 'So how does Anton earn money?' he asked.

'I'm not giving that away,' Dot told him. 'All I can tell you is that the poor boy is working day and night. He loves his mother, so he works and cooks and earns money to pay for the food and the rent, and when he gets his hair cut he pays for it in instalments. In fact I'm surprised he doesn't sleep right through all your lessons.' Mr Bremser was standing still while the other teachers listened. Dot was in full flow. 'And then you sit down and write his mother a letter saying her son is lazy! That beats everything. The shock will make the poor woman ill again at once if you send that letter. Maybe she'll get some more growths and have to go back to hospital because of you. And then, I can assure you, Anton will fall ill himself. He can't go on living like that much longer.'

Mr Bremser said, 'Don't be so cross. Why didn't he tell me about it?'

'You have a good point,' Dot agreed. 'That's what I asked him myself, and do you know what he said?'

'Well?' asked the teacher. And his colleagues had left their chairs again and were standing in a semicircle round the little girl.

'"I'd sooner bite my tongue off", that's what he said,' Dot told Mr Bremser. 'He's probably very proud.'

Mr Bremser moved away from the window sill. 'All right,' he said, 'I won't write the letter.'

'Good,' said Dot. 'You're a nice man. I thought so at once. Thank you very much.'

The teacher went to the door with her, 'It's for me to thank you too, my child.'

'And one more thing, before I forget,' said Dot. 'Please don't tell Anton that I came to see you.'

'I won't say a word,' Mr Bremser told her, patting her hand. Then the bell rang for lessons to begin again. Dot raced downstairs, got in the car with Mr Hollack, and he drove her home. She was rocking back and forth on the well-upholstered seat all the way and singing to herself.

ABOUT FRIENDSHIP

Let me tell you, whether you believe me or not, I envy Dot. People don't often get such a good chance to be useful to a friend as she did. And it's very unusual for them to be able to do someone a favour like that in secret! Mr Bremser won't be writing a letter to Anton's mother now. He won't be so hard on the boy any more. At first Anton will be astonished, then he'll be glad, and Dot will be secretly rubbing her hands with glee. She knows how it all happened. But for her, it wouldn't have worked.

But Anton won't know that. Dot doesn't need thanks, what she did is its own reward. Anything else would make her pleasure less rather than greater.

I hope every one of you will have a good friend. And I hope you all have the chance to do something nice for your friends without letting them know. Stick to finding out how happy it makes us to make other people happy!

Chapter Nine
Mrs Gast Has a Disappointment

While Anton was looking in his satchel for the key to the apartment, the door opened of itself, and there stood his mother. 'A good day for a nice meal, my boy!' she said, smiling.

'Yes, a good day for it,' he echoed her, puzzled. Then he risked jumping for joy, hugged her and said, 'I'm so glad you're better now.' They went into the living room. Anton sat on the sofa and was glad of every step his mother took. 'It's still rather a strain,' she admitted, sitting wearily down beside him. 'How was school today?'

'Richard Naumann said in geography that the Red Indians live in India. My goodness, he's stupid! And Schmitz pinched Pramann, and Pramann jumped up from the bench, and Mr Bremser asked what the matter was, and Pramann said he thought he must have a flea, maybe even two, and then Schmitz got up and objected to sitting next to boys who had fleas on them because his parents wouldn't like it. We laughed like anything.' And Anton himself laughed again, savouring the joke like an animal chewing the cud. Then he asked, 'Don't you like jokes today?'

'Oh, yes, do go on,' she said.

He put his head on the back of the sofa and stretched out his legs. 'Well, in the last lesson Mr Bremser was very nice to me, and he said I must go and see him when I had time.' Suddenly he gave a start. 'I'm an idiot!' he exclaimed. 'I must start cooking.' But his mother stopped him, and pointed to the table. There were plates on it already, and a large, steaming bowl of something.

'Lentils with sausages?' he asked. She nodded, and then they sat down and ate the lentils. Anton had a large helping, and when he had cleared his plate his mother gave him more. He nodded to her appreciatively. But then he noticed that her own helping was still untouched, and that made him lose his appetite. He pushed the lentils about his plate sadly, and fished out little sausages. Silence settled on the room like a menacing mist.

Finally he couldn't stand it any longer. 'Mama, did I do something wrong? Sometimes I don't know myself what to... Or is it because of the money? The sausages weren't really necessary.' He put his hand lovingly on hers.

But his mother quickly carried the dishes into the kitchen. Then she came back and said, 'You'd better begin your home-work. I'll be back soon.' He sat on his chair, shaking his head and wondering what the matter was. Outside, the door to the corridor closed. He opened the window, sat on the window sill and leant far out. It was some time before his mother came out into the street down below. She took small steps while she walked, because it tired her. She went down Artilleriestrasse and then turned the corner.

Feeling melancholy, he sat down at the table, opened his satchel, took the top off the bottle of ink, and began chewing the end of his pen-holder.

At last his mother came back. She had bought a little bunch of flowers, she fetched water, put the flowers in the vase with blue spots on it, arranged the leaves nicely, closed the window, turned her back to Anton and said nothing.

'Pretty flowers,' he said, clasping his hands. He could hardly breathe. 'They're cowslips, aren't they?'

His mother was standing in the room like a stranger. She looked out of the window and shrugged her shoulders. He felt like running to her, but he just got part of the way off his chair and begged her, 'Say something!' His voice was hoarse, and she probably didn't hear him.

Then she asked, without turning round, 'What date is it today?'

That surprised him, but so as not to annoy her even more he went over to the calendar on the wall and read out loud, 'April the ninth.'

'April the ninth,' she repeated, pressing her handkerchief to her mouth.

And suddenly he knew what had happened! It was his mother's birthday today, and he had forgotten.

He dropped back on his chair, trembling. He closed his eyes and wished he could die there and then... so that was why she had got up today. And that was why she had made lentils and sausages. She'd had to buy herself a bunch of flowers. And now she was standing by the window feeling all alone in the world. And he couldn't go over to her and have a cuddle, because she would never be able to forgive him for forgetting. If only at least he'd known how to fall ill very quickly. Then of course she'd have come to his bedside and been kind to him again. He stood up and went to the door, where he turned round once more and asked hopefully, 'Did you say something, Mama?'

However, she was leaning on the window sill, silent and motionless. He went out of the room, into the kitchen, sat down beside the stove and waited to begin crying. But no tears would come. Just sometimes, he shook as if someone were holding him by the collar.

Then he went to get his paintbox and took a mark out of it. There was no point in any of that now. He put the mark in his pocket. Could he run downstairs now and buy her a present? Then he'd be able to put it through the letter box and run away. And never come back again! Some chocolate and a birthday card would go through the flap of the letter box easily. He would write 'From your deeply unhappy son Anton' inside the card. Then his mother would at least have a good memory of him.

He stole out of the kitchen on tiptoe, went down the corridor, cautiously opened the handle of the front door and closed the door behind him like a thief.

His mother stood by the window for a long time, looking through the panes as if her poor, sad life lay spread out there before her. She had had nothing but trouble, nothing but illness and anxiety. There seemed to be a secret meaning in the fact that her son had forgotten her birthday. She was slowly losing him, too, just as she had lost everything else, and in that case her whole life had lost its meaning. When she had her operation, she had thought: I must stay alive, because what will become of Anton if I die? And now he had forgotten her birthday!

At last she felt pity for the little lad. Where could he be? He'd have been sorry for his forgetfulness long ago. He had asked, 'Did you say something, Mama?' before he sadly left the room. She mustn't be hard on him. He'd had such a shock. She mustn't be stern, when he'd put up with so much for her sake these last few weeks. First he had visited her every day in hospital. He'd had to eat in the soup kitchen run by a charity, and he'd been all alone in the apartment day and night. Then she had been brought home. She'd stayed in bed for two weeks, and Anton cooked and did the shopping, and he even cleaned round the room with a wet cloth now and then.

She began looking for him. She went into the bedroom. She went into the kitchen. She even tried the toilet. She put on the light in the corridor and investigated the space behind the cupboards. 'Anton!' she called. 'Come here, my dear, I'm not cross now! Anton!'

Sometimes she called his name in a loud voice, sometimes she called it in a soft, loving voice. He wasn't in the apartment.

He had run away! She felt terribly anxious. She called his name pleadingly. But he had gone.

He had gone! She flung the front door of the apartment open and ran downstairs to go in search of her boy.

ABOUT SELF-CONTROL

Do you like Anton? I like him very much, but to be honest I don't particularly like the way he ran off and left his mother on her own. Where would we be if everyone who did something wrong tried running away from it? It doesn't bear thinking of. You have to keep your head, not lose it!

It's the same in other ways as well. A boy gets bad marks at school, or his teacher writes his parents a letter, or a child accidentally breaks an expensive vase at home, and then we so often read in the paper: 'Ran away for fear of punishment. Isn't to be found anywhere. The parents dread the worst.'

No, ladies and gentlemen, that's not the way to act! If you've done something wrong, you have to pull yourself together and face the music. If you're so scared of punishment then you ought to have thought of that before.

Self-control is an important, valuable quality. And the especially remarkable thing about it is that you can learn self-control. Alexander the Great didn't want to be carried away into acting without thinking, so he always counted up to thirty before doing anything. That's a very good idea. You should do the same if necessary.

It would be an even better idea to count up to sixty.

Chapter Ten
Things Could Go Wrong

'Hello, Mrs Gast,' someone said to Mrs Gast as she came out of the building. 'You're looking wonderful.' It was Dot, with Piefke, and in fact Dot thought that Anton's mother looked shockingly pale and upset. However, the boy had asked her to say how good his mother looked, and she was a girl who kept her word, wasn't she just! Miss Andacht was at the Café Sommerlatte with her fiancé, and she had told Dot to meet her there at six o'clock precisely.

Mrs Gast looked around her, distraught, and gave Dot her hand without saying a word.

'Where's Anton?' the child asked.

'Gone!' whispered Mrs Gast. 'Oh dear, just think, he's run away. I was upset because he forgot it was my birthday.'

'Many happy returns,' said Dot. 'Of your birthday, I mean.'

'Thank you,' Mrs Gast replied. 'Oh, where can he be?'

'Don't lose your head,' Dot consoled her. 'We'll find him. They say a bad penny always turns up. Suppose we go to the shops and ask in all of them?' And as Anton's mother didn't seem to be listening, Dot took her hand and led her to the dairy on the ground floor of the next building. Then she put her dachshund down in the street and told him, 'Good dog! Go and find Anton. Seek!' But yet again it turned out that Piefke didn't understand human language.

Meanwhile, Anton was buying chocolate.

The saleswoman was an old lady with an enormous goitre under her chin. She looked at him suspiciously as, with a totally miserable expression on his face, he asked for a bar of the best milk chocolate.

'It's for a birthday present,' he said gloomily.

She got a little friendlier then, gift-wrapped the chocolate beautifully in tissue paper and tied a pale blue silk ribbon round it. 'Thank you very much indeed,' he said in a serious voice, and he carefully put the chocolate bar in his pocket and paid. She gave him change, and he went into the stationer's shop next door.

In the stationer's shop, he chose a card from the birthday card album. It was a beautiful card, with a picture of a stout commissionaire smiling cheerfully on it, and the stout commissionaire was holding a large pot of flowers in the crook of each arm. Golden lettering at his feet said: 'All good wishes for your happiness on your birthday.'

Anton looked sadly at the lovely picture. Then he went behind the desk where you could write your own message, and added on the back, in his best and most laborious handwriting, 'From your deeply unhappy son Anton. Please forgive me, dear Mama, I didn't mean to hurt you.' Then he pushed the card under the blue ribbon round the gift-wrapped chocolate bar and hurried out into the street. At this point he was feeling very emotional because of his own sad fate. He was afraid that he was going to cry, but he bravely swallowed his tears and went on, his head bowed.

Once inside the building he felt very frightened. He made his way up to the fourth floor like an Indian on the warpath. On tiptoe, he went over to the door of the apartment. He raised the flap of the letter box and put his present through it. It made a noise as it dropped, and his heart thumped.

But nothing inside the apartment moved.

At this point he ought really to have run away to die somewhere as fast as possible. But he couldn't do it just like that, so he hesitantly pressed the doorbell. Then he ran to the landing of the next staircase along and waited, holding his breath. Still nothing moved inside the apartment.

He ventured to go back to the door again. He rang the bell once more. And then he ran downstairs again.

And still there wasn't a sound to be heard! What was the matter with his mother? Had something happened to her? Had she fallen ill again because she was so worried about him? Was she lying in bed, unable to move? He hadn't taken his keys with him. Perhaps she had turned on the gas to kill herself in her grief? He ran back to the door and clattered the flap of the letter box. He banged on the door with both fists. He called through the keyhole. 'Mama! Mama! It's me. Open the door!'

Still nothing stirred inside the apartment.

He fell to his knees on the straw matting, sobbing. Now it was all over.

Anton's mother and Dot had asked all the shopkeepers who knew Anton. The milkman, the baker, the butcher, the greengrocer, the cobbler, the plumber—none of them had seen him.

Dot ran over to the traffic policeman on duty at the cross-roads and asked him. But he just shook his head and went on waving his arms at the cars. All that waving annoyed Dot. She squealed. Meanwhile Mrs Gast was waiting on the pavement, looking anxiously at everything around them. 'No luck,' said Dot. 'I tell you what, I think we'd better go back to your home.'

But Mrs Gast didn't move.

'He could be down in the cellar,' said the child.

'The cellar?' repeated Anton's mother.

'Yes, or up in the attic,' Dot suggested.

And they ran over the road as fast as they could and back into the apartment building. Just as Mrs Gast was about to open the cellar door, she heard someone sobbing upstairs.

'That's him!' cried Dot.

Anton's mother was laughing and crying at the same time. She ran up the stairs so fast that Dot could hardly keep up with her. 'Anton!' cried his mother.

And his voice replied, from higher up, 'Mama! Mama!' Then a great race began, one of them running upstairs and the other downstairs. Dot stayed where she was on the first floor. She didn't want to be in the way, and she held Piefke's muzzle shut to keep him quiet.

Mother and son met halfway on the stairs and fell into each other's arms. They couldn't stop hugging and kissing, they were so glad to be back together again. They sat on the stairs, holding hands and smiling. They were both very tired, and couldn't think of anything but how happy they were. At last Anton's mother said, 'Come along, my boy, we can't sit here for ever. Suppose someone saw us.'

'No, that would never do. They wouldn't understand,' said Anton. They climbed the rest of the stairs together, hand in hand. When his mother had unlocked the door and gone into the living room with him, Anton whispered in her ear, 'Look in the letter box.'

She looked, clapped her hands, and cried, 'Oh, someone's been here to leave me a birthday card!'

'Really?' he said, giving her a big hug and wishing her a very happy birthday and many, many happy returns. She secretly read the back of the beautiful birthday card while she was making coffee. She cried a little, but it was out of sheer happiness.

Then the doorbell rang. Mrs Gast opened the door. 'Oh, goodness, I quite forgot you!'

'Let me wish you many happy returns of the day again,' said Dot. 'May we come in?' Then Anton came along to say hello to her and the dachshund. 'Honestly, you'll give me white hairs!' Dot told him reproachfully. 'We searched everywhere for you.

It was like looking for a needle in a haystack.' She rubbed noses with him. Then his mother came into the living room with the coffee pot, and they all drank coffee. There wasn't any birthday cake, but the three of them were very happy all the same. And Piefke barked a little song for the birthday girl.

After coffee, Anton's mother told the children, 'You have a little walk. I'm going to bed. All this excitement has been rather too much for my first full day up and about. I shall sleep wonderfully well tonight.'

On the stairs, Anton told Dot, 'I won't be forgetting today in a hurry.'

THE TENTH AFTERTHOUGHT IS:

ABOUT FAMILY HAPPINESS

Grown-ups have their own troubles. Children have their own troubles too. And sometimes the troubles are more than the children and the grown-ups can cope with, and because they are so big and broad those troubles cast many, many shadows. So the parents and their children sit in the shade of their troubles and feel freezing cold. Then, if a child goes to his father and asks a question, the father growls, 'Leave me alone! I'm busy thinking!' So the child goes away, and the father hides behind his newspaper. And if the mother comes into the room and asks, 'What's the matter?' they both say, 'Oh, nothing to speak of,' and family happiness turns to vinegar. Or sometimes the parents quarrel, or like Dot's parents they're never at home, and they hand their children over to strangers, for instance people like Miss Andacht. Or someone else, and then...

As I was writing that, I suddenly realized that this afterthought really ought to be read by grown-ups. So next time there's trouble at home, open the book at this page and give it to your parents to read, will you? That never does anyone any harm.

Chapter Eleven

Mr Pogge
Practises Spying

When Mr Pogge the director came home in the evening, Gottfried Klepperbein met him at the front door of the building. 'Oh, your coat's all dirty at the back, sir,' he said. 'Just a moment.' Dot's father stopped, and the caretaker's son brushed down the back of his coat, although it wasn't dirty at all. That was the boy's favourite trick, and it had already earned him a lot of money. 'There,' he said, holding out his hand. Mr Pogge gave him a small coin and was going on into the building, but Gottfried Klepperbein stood in his way. 'I could give you a hint well worth ten marks,' he offered.

'Let me by, please,' said Mr Pogge.

'It's about the young lady your daughter,' whispered Gottfried Klepperbein, and he winked.

'Well, what about her?'

'Ten marks, or I'm not saying another word,' the boy told him, holding out his hand again.

'I pay only on delivery of the goods,' said Dot's father.

'Word of honour?' asked the boy.

'What? Oh, I see. Very well, word of honour.'

'Are you going out again this evening?'

'We're going to the opera,' said Mr Pogge.

'Then pretend to leave,' Gottfried Klepperbein told him, 'but wait here outside the building, and if you don't get the surprise of your life a quarter of an hour later then Bob's your uncle!'

'All right,' said Mr Pogge, and he pushed past the boy and went into the building.

Before Dot's parents left for the opera house they went to her room, as usual. Dot was in bed, and Miss Andacht was reading her the story of *Aladdin and his Wonderful Lamp*.

Dot's mother shook her head. 'A big girl like you, still having fairy tales read to her!'

'Fairy tales are so exciting and magical, and so peculiar too,' said Dot. 'I love them!'

'Well, yes,' said her father, 'but they're not exactly the right thing to read before you go to sleep.'

'I have strong nerves, you see, Director,' claimed his daughter.

'Sleep well, darling,' said Dot's mother. This evening she was wearing silver shoes, a little silvery hat and a blue dress trimmed with lace.

'Good wet,' said Dot.

'What?' asked her mother.

'It's going to rain,' said the child. 'I have rheumatism in my nightie.'

'It's raining already,' said her mother.

'There you are then,' Dot pointed out. 'My rheumatism is always right.'

Mr Pogge asked Miss Andacht whether she was going out herself later.

'Goodness me, no, sir,' she replied.

When his wife was in the car, he said, 'Give me my ticket, will you? I forgot to bring my cigars. You go on ahead, Hollack, and I'll follow in a taxi.'

Mrs Pogge looked curiously at her husband and gave him one of their tickets. He waved to the chauffeur, and the car drove away.

Of course Mr Pogge didn't go back to the apartment. He was not the sort of man to forget his cigars. He got behind a tree opposite the building and waited. He thought it was rather silly of him to fall for that boy's strange ideas, and he felt ashamed of it. On the other hand, he'd had a funny feeling in the pit of his stomach for several days.

So, in short, he waited. Thin rain was falling. The street was deserted, except for a car driving past now and then. Mr Pogge the director couldn't remember ever standing in the rain waiting for something mysterious to happen before.

He took a cigar out of his cigar case. Then it occurred to him that the glowing end of a cigar would give him away in the dark, so he kept it clenched between his teeth, unlit. Suppose someone he knew saw him now! What a sensational scandal that would be! 'Fancy Pogge the well-known businessman

standing on the watch outside his own apartment,' people would say.

He looked up at the windows of the building. There was still a light on in Dot's room. So much for the boy's ideas.

There! The light went out!

Why was he getting worked up like this? Dot had probably gone to sleep, and the governess would be back in her own room. All the same, his heart was beating faster. He peered through the dim light at the front door of the building.

And then it opened! Mr Pogge bit his lower lip, almost swallowing the cigar. A woman's figure slipped out, leading a child behind her. The two of them moved like ghosts in the darkness. The front door closed. The woman looked around in concern. Mr Pogge kept close to the tree. Then the woman and the child ran off towards the city centre.

Perhaps they were total strangers? Mr Pogge the director followed them on the other side of the street. He was out of breath, and kept his hand over his mouth. He stepped in puddles, brushed against lamp posts and hardly noticed when one of his sock suspenders gave way. The other two had no idea that they were being shadowed. The child stumbled, and the tall, thin woman dragged her on. Suddenly they stopped, just before the quiet street merged with the traffic of the big city.

Mr Pogge, on tiptoe, went a little farther. What was going on over there? He couldn't see properly. He was afraid the couple might get away from him. He kept his eyes wide open and tried not to blink, as if they might disappear from the face of the earth if he lowered his lids even for a second.

But no, the two figures, the woman and the child, came out of the shadows of the quiet buildings and made for the bright lights of the next street. The woman had put a headscarf on. She was walking very slowly, and now the little girl was leading the woman as if she suddenly felt ill. Although there was such a crowd of people going along the street here, Mr Pogge could follow them easily. They passed Friedrichstrasse Station and went towards the Weidendammer Bridge.

And, once on the bridge, they stopped, leaning against the balustrade.

It was still raining.

ABOUT TELLING LIES

Dot tells her parents lies, there's no denying it. And, nice as she is otherwise, it's not right for her to be a liar. Suppose we had her here now, and we asked, 'Aren't you ashamed of yourself? Why do you lie to your parents?' what would she say? As it happens, she's standing on the Weidendammer Bridge, so we can't disturb her. But what would she say if she were here with us? 'It's Miss Andacht's fault,' that's what she would say, and that would be a poor excuse.

Because if you don't want to tell a lie, no power on earth can make you do it. Perhaps Dot is afraid of the governess? Perhaps Miss Andacht has threatened the child?

In that case, Dot would only have to go to her father and say, 'Director, the governess is trying to make me tell you and Mama lies.' Then Miss Andacht would be dismissed on the spot, and her threat would have been for nothing.

There's no denying it: Dot tells lies, which is not right. Let's hope that she will learn from experience and never tell lies again in future.

Chapter Twelve

Klepperbein Earns Ten Marks and a Punch in the Face

Mr Pogge was standing in the middle of the street outside the opera house, straining his eyes as he looked at the Weidendammer Bridge. He saw the child holding out her hands to passers-by and bobbing curtseys at the same time. Sometimes the passers-by stopped and gave her some money. Then the little girl curtseyed again and seemed to be saying thank you. He remembered yesterday's scene at home. Dot had been standing in the living room, complaining to the wall of her sad fate and saying, 'Matches, buy my matches, ladies and gentlemen!' She had been rehearsing! There was no possible doubt about it: his child was standing over there begging! A cold shiver ran down his spine.

He looked at the tall, thin woman with her. Miss Andacht, of course. She was wearing a headscarf and a pair of dark glasses. He hardly recognized her.

There was his child on the bridge in an old, thin dress and no hat, her hair wet with the rain. He turned up his coat collar.

As he did so, he realized that he was still holding the cold cigar between his fingers. It was shredded to bits, and he angrily threw it into a puddle, as if it were to blame for everything. Then a policeman came along and told him to walk on the pavement.

'Officer,' said Mr Pogge, 'are small children allowed to stand here at night begging?'

The police officer shrugged his shoulders. 'You mean those two on the bridge? What can we do about it? Who else would lead the blind woman around?'

'Blind, is she?'

'Yes, of course. And still quite young, too. They stand over there almost every evening. Such people want to live as well.' The policeman was surprised to find that the strange gentleman was gripping his arm quite painfully. Then he said, 'Yes, it's a real shame.'

'How long do the two of them usually stay there?'

'At least two hours, until about ten.'

Mr Pogge got off the pavement again. His face looked as if he were going to fall over, but then he controlled himself and thanked the policeman, who saluted him and went away.

Suddenly there was Gottfried Klepperbein, grinning all over his face and plucking at Mr Pogge's coat, 'Well, what did I tell you, sir?' he whispered. 'Wasn't I right?'

Mr Pogge said nothing, but stared across the street.

'And your daughter's boyfriend is over there on the other side of the bridge. He's begging too, but he does it for real. Anton Gast is his name. He ought to have been in some kind of home long ago.'

Mr Pogge still said nothing, and looked at Anton. So Dot was friends with a beggar boy, was she? And just why were his daughter and her governess selling matches? What was behind all this? Why did they secretly need money? He didn't know what to think.

'So now you owe me my ten marks,' said Gottfried Klepperbein, pawing at Mr Pogge's coat. The director took out his wallet and gave the boy a ten-mark note.

'Don't put your wallet away yet,' said Klepperbein. 'If you give me another ten marks I won't tell anyone what you've seen. Otherwise I'll go round telling everyone, and it'll be in the newspaper tomorrow. I'm sure that would be embarrassing for you.'

At this point Mr Pogge's patience snapped. He gave the boy a resounding punch in the face. Some of the passers-by stopped and were going to intervene, but the lad ran away so fast that they thought the gentleman must have good reasons for hitting him. Gottfried Klepperbein ran as fast as his legs would carry him. The story was earning him rather too many punches. This one made three, and he decided to be content with his ten marks. Ten marks, three punches—he'd had enough for the time being.

Mr Pogge couldn't bear to watch his child standing on the bridge in the rain any longer. Should he go over to Dot and bring her home? But then he had what he thought was a better idea. He hailed a taxi. 'Drive as fast as you can to the State Opera House on Unter den Linden,' he told the driver as he got in, and away they went.

What was his plan?

Anton wasn't doing good business tonight. For one thing, he was on the wrong side of the street again, and for another it was raining. In the rain people walked over the bridge even faster than usual, and they didn't feel like stopping and taking out their wallets or purses. So business was bad, but he was in a good mood. He was so glad to be friends with his mother again.

Suddenly he gave a little start. Surely that was Miss Andacht's fiancé over there, Robert the Devil? Wearing a raincoat, with a cap pulled far down over his face, he walked past Anton without noticing him.

The man went to the end of the bridge, where he crossed it and walked slowly back on the other side. Anton stared. Any moment now the man would reach Miss Andacht. Anton himself moved slowly along beside the balustrade. Now the man gave Dot's governess a signal, and she twitched with fright. Dot didn't notice anything. She was curtseying and wailing and doing her best to sell matches to all the passers-by.

When he was only a little way from the three of them, Anton stood close to the balustrade and watched what happened next. The man dug Miss Andacht in the ribs. She shook her head, and then he grabbed her arm, put his hand in the bag hanging over it, rummaged around in the bag and brought out something shiny. Anton looked keenly at it—it was a bunch of keys.

Keys? Why was the man getting keys from Miss Andacht?

The man turned round, and Anton leant over the balustrade of the bridge to avoid being noticed and spat into the river. The man passed him, and now he suddenly seemed to be in a great hurry. He went down Schiffbauerdamm.

Anton didn't stop to think about it for long. He walked into the first restaurant he came to, asked to see the telephone book and looked under P. Then he took a coin out of his pocket and hurried into a telephone kiosk.

ABOUT NASTY PIECES OF WORK

Gottfried Klepperbein is a nasty piece of work. Representatives of this species of the human race aren't always grown-ups, but may be children, and that's particularly painful. There's a whole series of signs that someone is a nasty piece of work. If a person is lazy and at the same time enjoys other people's bad luck, is malicious and greedy, if he's always after money and tells lies, then ten to one he's a nasty piece of work. Making a nasty piece of work like that into a decent human being is about the most difficult job anyone can face. Carrying water in a sieve is child's play by comparison. I wonder why? If you tell someone how nice it is to be a decent human being, and how good it would make him feel, surely he'd try hard to be like that, don't you think?

There are such things as extending telescopes. Have you seen one? They look nice and small, and can easily fit into your pocket. But they can also be fully extended, and then they're over half a metre long. It seems to me that nasty pieces of work are like that. Or maybe people in general are like that. As children they're already much the same as they will be later. Like the extending telescopes. They only grow, they don't change. If something isn't in a human being from the first, then you can't get it out of him, and if you turn that idea upside down, then ...

Chapter Thirteen

Fat Berta Swings the Clubs

Fat Berta was sitting in the kitchen, eating a liver sausage sandwich and drinking coffee. She had been for a walk with her friend, because it was her day off, but because the rain didn't stop she was home again earlier than usual. Now she was enjoying some liver sausage to make up for the rainy day off, and reading the novel in her illustrated magazine. Suddenly the telephone rang. 'Oh no!' she muttered, and she shuffled off to answer it. 'This is Director Pogge's residence,' she said.

'Can I speak to the director, please?' asked a child's voice.

'No,' said Berta. 'Mr and Mrs Pogge are at the opera.'

'Oh dear, this is terrible,' said the child.

'What's it about, if I may ask?' said Berta.

'Who's speaking?'

'I'm the Pogge family's maid.'

'Oh, fat Berta!' cried the child.

'Less of the *fat*, if you don't mind,' she said, offended, 'but yes, I'm Berta.'

'I'm a friend of Dot's,' said the child's voice.

'Oh yes?' said Berta. 'And I suppose you want me to go to her room in the middle of the night and ask if she'd like to play football with you?'

'No, nonsense!' said the boy. 'Only the fact is that Miss Andacht's fiancé will be at the Pogges' apartment any time now.'

'This gets better and better!' said Berta. 'The governess will have been asleep for ages.'

'Not a bit of it,' said the child's voice. 'There's no one there except you.'

Fat Berta stared at the telephone receiver as if it would tell her whether this was true. 'What?' she asked. 'What? You mean Miss Andacht and Dot aren't in their beds?'

'No, they aren't,' cried the child. 'I'll explain it to you some other time. You're all alone at home. Do please believe me. And now the fiancé is on his way to break in. He already has the keys. And a plan of the apartment as well. He'll arrive any moment.'

'Oh, delightful,' said Berta. 'What am I supposed to do about it?'

'Call the police, quick. And then find a coal shovel or something like that. And when the fiancé arrives, hit him over the head with it.'

'It's all very well for you to talk, sonny boy,' said Berta.

'Good luck!' cried the child. 'Do your best. Don't forget to call the police. See you soon!'

What with the way she was shaking her head and the way her teeth were chattering, Berta could hardly move from the spot. She was badly upset. She rattled the handle of Dot's door, and then she tried Miss Andacht's door. Not a soul at home. No one was stirring, except for Piefke, who barked a bit. He was in his basket outside Dot's door, but he got out of it and followed Berta. She pulled herself together and called the police.

'Okay,' said the policeman who answered the phone. 'I'll send some men round right away.'

Then Berta went looking for a weapon. 'What makes the boy think of a coal shovel when we have central heating?' she asked Piefke. At last she found two wooden clubs in the child's room. Dot sometimes did exercises with them. She took one of the clubs, stationed herself beside the door into the corridor, and put out the corridor light.

'We'll leave the light in the kitchen on,' she told Piefke. 'Or I might miss when I hit him.' Piefke lay down beside her and waited patiently. He wasn't quite in the picture, and growled at his own tail as he lay there.

'Shut up!' whispered Berta. Piefke couldn't stand that tone of voice, but he obeyed. Berta fetched a chair and sat down, because she wasn't feeling very strong. Everything was topsy-turvy today. Where could Miss Andacht and Dot be? Oh, bother it, if only she'd said something sooner!

Then someone came up the stairs outside the apartment. She got to her feet, picked up the club and held her breath. The Someone was outside the front door. Piefke stood up and arched his back like a cat. His coat was standing on end.

The Someone put the key in the lock and turned it. Then he put the yale key in its lock and turned that too. Then he

activated the mortice lock, and the door sprang open. The Someone stepped into the corridor and the dim light from the kitchen. Berta raised her club and hit the man over the head with it. He staggered and fell heavily to the floor.

'Got him,' Berta told Piefke, putting on the light. She had knocked out a man in a raincoat, with a cap pulled well down over his face. Piefke sniffed at Miss Andacht's fiancé and suddenly, if too late in the day, he became very brave and bit the man's calf. But the man went on lying on the coconut-matting runner in the corridor and didn't move.

'I wish the police would hurry up,' said Berta. She sat on her chair again, picked up the club and kept her eye on the man. 'We ought to tie him up,' she told Piefke. 'Go and find a washing line in the kitchen, will you?' Piefke coughed as if he were saying something. They were both sitting beside the intruder, afraid that he might come back to his senses.

There! The man opened his eyes, which were getting clearer, and struggled to sit up.

'I'm terribly sorry,' said fat Berta, with much feeling, and hit him over the head again. The man sighed slightly and collapsed once more.

'Where on earth are the police?' said Berta crossly.

But then the forces of law and order arrived, three of them, and they couldn't help laughing at the sight that met their eyes.

'I wish I knew what's so funny about it,' snapped fat Berta. 'Tie the man up, why don't you? He's going to come round any minute now.' So the police officers put handcuffs on the intruder and searched him. They found the keys, the plan of the apartment, a set of skeleton keys and a revolver. The sergeant took charge of these items. Berta gave the three officers coffee in the kitchen and asked them to wait until the Pogges came home. Their daughter and the daughter's governess had disappeared, she added, and who knew what else had been going on today?

'Right, we'll wait, but only for a few minutes,' said the sergeant.

Soon they were all in the middle of a lively conversation. Meanwhile Piefke guarded the handcuffed villain, and secretly found out what the soles of his shoes tasted like.

ABOUT CHANCE

If it hadn't rained that evening, fat Berta would have come home later. If fat Berta had come home later, the thief could have burgled the apartment undisturbed. It was pure chance that she was at home and the burglary failed. If Galvani hadn't happened to notice two dead frogs' legs twitching, then animal electricity wouldn't have been discovered, or not until much later.

If Napoleon hadn't been so tired on 18th October 1813, he might have won the Battle of Leipzig.

Many events that have decided the course of human history came about by chance, and the opposite or something completely different could just as well have happened.

Chance is the greatest of all the great powers in the world.

Other people call it not chance, but fate or providence. They say it was a dispensation of providence that Napoleon felt so tired on 18th October 1813, and had such a bad stomach ache. Chance or fate—it's a matter of taste. In such cases my mother says: some like to eat sausage, some like to eat green soap, take your pick.

Chapter Fourteen

An Evening Dress Gets Grubby

Mr Pogge the director jumped out of his cab in front of the Unter den Linden opera house, paid the driver and hurried into the theatre. His wife was sitting in a box, listening to the music with her eyes half closed. The show tonight was *La Bohème*, a very beautiful opera. Its music sounds like a shower of delicious sweets. An extremely famous tenor was singing the part of Rodolfo, and seats in the boxes were shockingly expensive. Anton and his mother could have lived for two weeks on the price of Mr and Mrs Pogge's tickets for the opera.

Mr Pogge went into the box. His wife opened her eyes in surprise, and looked angrily at him. He placed himself behind her seat, took her by the shoulders and said, 'Come on out.' She didn't like the hard grip of his hands, and turned her indignant face to him. He was standing in dim light, wet through with rain, his coat collar turned up, and he was looking past her.

She had never felt much respect for her husband because he was too good to her. But now she felt afraid of him. 'What's all this about?' she asked.

'Come out at once!' he ordered. And when she still hesitated, he hauled her out of her seat and out of the box behind him. She could hardly believe what he was doing, but she didn't dare to contradict him any more. She hurried down the stairs, followed by Mr Pogge, who asked where the ladies' cloakroom was and put her cape round her shoulders. He stamped his foot impatiently as she looked at herself in the mirror and adjusted her little silvery hat. Then he dragged her out of the opera house. Mr Hollack the chauffeur wasn't there, of course; he wasn't expecting to meet them until the end of the performance. Mr Pogge didn't let go of his wife's hand. He stumbled through the puddles and across the street with her. She could have cried with vexation. There were some taxis at the corner of the street; he pushed his wife into the first, told the driver where to go, and got in after her. Then he sat on her silk cape, but she didn't dare to say so.

The car drove very fast. Mr Pogge sat hunched beside his wife with an absent-minded expression on his face, shifting his feet nervously.

'My silver shoes are ruined,' she murmured. 'We left my over-shoes in the cloakroom.'

He didn't reply, but stared straight ahead. How did Miss Andacht, dressed in rags and apparently blind, come to be begging by night with his child? Was the woman out of her mind? 'Stupid creature!' he said.

'Who's a stupid creature?' asked his wife.

She got no answer.

'What's all this about?' she asked. 'There am I just sitting in the theatre, and you drag me out into the rain. It was an excellent performance, too. And think what the tickets cost!'

'Be quiet!' he replied, looking through the car window. The taxi stopped outside the Comic Opera House, and they got out. Mrs Pogge looked at her soaked shoes in despair. To think she'd left her over-shoes behind in the theatre cloak-room! Miss Andacht would have to go and pick them up in the morning.

'There!' whispered her husband, pointing to the Weidendammer Bridge.

She saw cars, cyclists, a traffic policeman, a beggar woman with a child, a newspaper boy with an umbrella, and one of the buses where a ticket cost five pfennigs came past. She shrugged her shoulders.

Mr Pogge took her arm and carefully led her towards the bridge. 'Watch that beggar woman and the child,' he whispered commandingly.

She saw the little girl bobbing curtseys, offering boxes of matches to the passers-by and taking money from them. Suddenly she gave a start of alarm, looked at her husband and said, 'Dot?'

They went closer. 'Dot!' whispered Mrs Pogge, unable to believe what her own eyes were seeing.

'My mother is totally blind, and still so young. Three boxes for twenty-five pfennigs. God bless you, kind lady,' the child was saying.

Yes, it was Dot! Mrs Pogge ran towards her child, who was freezing and bobbing curtseys in the rain. In spite of the wet,

dirty street she knelt down in front of the little girl and flung her arms round her. 'My child!' she cried, beside herself.

Dot was scared to death. What terrible luck! And her mother's dress was a shocking sight. The people on the bridge stopped and stared, thinking that someone was making a film.

Mr Pogge the director snatched the dark glasses off the blind woman's face.

'Miss Andacht!' cried the horrified Mrs Pogge.

Miss Andacht was as white as a sheet. She put her hands protectively in front of her face, completely at a loss. A policeman appeared.

'Sergeant!' cried Mr Pogge. 'Arrest this woman! She is our daughter's governess, and when we're not at home she takes the child begging with her!'

The policeman produced his notebook. The newspaper boy with the umbrella laughed.

'Don't lock me up!' cried Miss Andacht. 'Don't lock me up!' With a great leap, she broke through the circle of people watching and ran for all she was worth.

Mr Pogge was going to follow her, but the bystanders held him back.

'Let the girl go!' one old man said.

Mrs Pogge had got to her feet and was scrubbing away with a small lace-edged handkerchief at her silk dress, which was terribly grubby.

Then Anton came over from the other side of the street and put his hand on Dot's shoulder. 'What's going on?' he asked.

'My parents have caught me,' Dot told him quietly, 'and Miss Andacht has just run away. I'm in real trouble.'

'Will they do anything nasty to you?' he asked, worried.

'I don't know yet,' Dot said, shrugging her shoulders.

'Shall I help you?' he asked.

'Oh, yes,' she said. 'Stay here. That makes me feel better.'

Mr Pogge was talking to the policeman. His wife was still trying to clean her expensive dress. The people who had been standing around went their own ways again.

Then Mrs Pogge looked up, saw her daughter talking to a strange boy and grabbed hold of the child. 'You come with me this minute!' she cried. 'Why are you talking to this beggar boy?'

'That takes the biscuit!' said Anton. 'I'm as good as you any day. Just so as you know. And if you didn't happen to be my friend's mother I wouldn't even speak to you, understand?'

Mr Pogge the director noticed what was going on and went over to them.

'This is my best friend,' said Dot, taking his hand. 'His name is Anton, and he's splendid!'

'Really?' asked her father, amused.

'Splendid is going too far,' said Anton modestly. 'But I don't like people calling me names.'

'My wife didn't mean it like that,' Mr Pogge explained.

'I should just about hope not,' said Dot proudly, smiling at her friend. 'Now, let's go home. What do you say? Anton, are you coming with us?'

Anton said no, because he had to get back to his mother.

'Then will you come to see me after school tomorrow?'

'Fine,' said Anton, shaking her hand. 'If your parents are happy about that.'

'By all means,' said Dot's father, nodding.

Anton made a little bow and hurried away.

'Anton is wonderful,' said Dot, watching him go. Then they took a taxi home. Dot sat between her parents, playing with coins and matchboxes.

'How did all this come to happen?' her father asked sternly.

'Miss Andacht has a fiancé,' Dot told him. 'And he always needed money, so she kept coming here with me. We earned pretty well, too. I can say so without exaggerating.'

'But this is terrible, sweetheart,' cried her mother.

'What do you mean, terrible?' asked Dot. 'It was tremendously exciting.'

Mrs Pogge looked at her husband, shook her head and said, 'I ask you! Servants!'

THE FOURTEENTH AFTERTHOUGHT IS:

ABOUT RESPECT

There's a sentence in the last chapter that deserves another look. It says that 'Mrs Pogge had never felt much respect for her husband because he was too good to her.'

Can you ever be too good to people? Yes, I think so. Where I was born, we had a saying that someone was stupidly good. It meant that sheer kindness and friendliness can make you stupid, and that's wrong. Children are the first to know when someone is too good to them. If they've done something that they think deserved punishment, and they aren't punished, they wonder why not. And if the same thing happens again, they gradually lose respect for the person who doesn't punish them.

Respect is very important. Some children almost always do the right thing of their own accord, but most of them have to learn it first. And to learn it they need a barometer. They have to be able to feel: oh dear, what I just did was wrong, I deserve to be punished for it.

But if they don't get punished or told off, if they still get chocolate even though they were cheeky, they may think: I might as well always be cheeky because I'll get chocolate all the same.

Respect is necessary, and so are people who can be respected, as long as children, and we human beings in general, aren't perfect.

Chapter Fifteen

A Policeman Dances the Tango

When they were going up the stairs of the apartment building, they heard gramophone music playing on the first floor. 'Hello?' said Mr Pogge, and he unlocked the door. Then he immediately turned into a pillar of salt, and his wife turned into another. Only Dot was not particularly surprised, but she was talking to Piefke the dog, who ran towards her.

Fat Berta was dancing the tango with a policeman in the corridor. Another policeman stood beside the big gramophone, turning its handle.

'Good heavens, Berta,' cried the horrified Mrs Pogge.

Dot went over to the policeman standing by the gramophone, bobbed him a curtsey and said, 'Ladies' request dance, Sergeant.'

The policeman put his arm round her waist, and they did a round of honour.

'Right, that's enough!' cried the director. 'Berta, what does all this mean? Are you engaged to a whole troop of police officers?'

'Unfortunately not,' said fat Berta. Then a third policeman came out of the kitchen, and Mrs Pogge murmured, 'I must be losing my wits.'

Dot stood in front of her and said, 'Oh, come on, Mama, join in!'

'We don't need her now,' said Berta, which wasn't really very polite of her, but Mrs Pogge didn't catch what she said, and her husband was busy shaking hands with everyone.

At last Berta led her employers into the kitchen, where they saw a man in a raincoat with handcuffs on his wrists.

'This man was going to break in,' said Berta, 'so I hit him on the head and called the police. And because you weren't here we thought we'd have a little dance.'

The man in handcuffs was just opening his glazed eyes.

'Why, that's Robert the Devil!' cried Dot.

Her parents looked at her in surprise. 'Who?'

'Miss Andacht's fiancé! So that's why she asked me when Berta had her day off!'

Mr Pogge said, 'And that's why the pair of you had to go out begging then.'

'And that's why she drew a plan of the apartment,' said Dot.

'We found it on him,' said one of the policemen, handing a piece of paper to the astonished master of the house.

'But how did you overpower him?' asked Mrs Pogge.

Fat Berta picked up the wooden club and went over to the door. 'I stood here, and when he unlocked the door and peered round it I bopped him on the head. Then he looked like coming back to his senses, so I bopped him on the head again. And then these three gallant gentlemen turned up.'

She pointed to the three police officers, who felt greatly flattered.

Dot's father was shaking his head again. 'I don't understand the first thing about all this,' he said. 'How did you know someone wanted to break into the apartment? Suppose it had been me coming home?'

'Then you'd have been bopped on the head yourself!' cried Dot, relishing the idea.

Berta explained, although in a rather confusing way. 'When I got back, it had been such a terribly rainy day, so I thought why walk round in the rain, and when I was sitting in the kitchen the telephone rings. Someone on the other end of the line says there's a burglar coming to break in, and tells me to hit him over the head with the coal shovel and call the police. Only we don't have a coal shovel. That's how it was.'

'But who knew that the man was going to break in here? Who telephoned to tell you?'

'Easy-peasy,' said Dot. 'That was my friend Anton, of course.'

'Right,' said Berta. 'He didn't introduce himself by name, but he said he was Dot's friend.'

'So there you are,' Dot pointed out, crossing her arms behind her back and stalking up and down the corridor. 'I told you just now, that boy is wonderful.'

'It certainly strikes me that you're right,' said Dot's father, lighting himself a cigar. 'But how did he know the man was on his way?'

'Maybe he saw Miss Andacht giving the keys to the thief,' said Dot.

Robert the Devil was shifting back and forth on his chair. 'So that was it,' he said. 'Just let that boy wait till I get my hands on him.'

'You can put that off until later,' said the police sergeant, 'because you'll be serving time behind bars first.'

Dot went over to the man. 'Let me advise you not to do it anyway,' she said, 'because Anton will make mincemeat of you. He punched Gottfried Klepperbein in the face twice and landed him on the floor.'

'Did he indeed?' asked her father, pleased. 'Yes, your friend Anton really is a splendid fellow.'

Piefke was sitting in front of the thief, pulling at his shoe-laces. Mrs Pogge got a migraine. She made a face to show how she was suffering. 'All this excitement has been too much for me,' she complained. 'Gentlemen, won't you take this burglar away? He's getting on my nerves.'

'And she's getting on mine,' muttered Robert the Devil. But then the police officers left, taking him with them.

'Dear Berta,' said Mrs Pogge, 'put the child to bed, please. I'm going to get some sleep. Will you be coming to bed soon, Fritz? Goodnight, sweetheart. And don't you ever play such tricks on us again.' She gave Dot a big kiss and went to her own room.

Suddenly Mr Pogge seemed very downcast. 'I'll put the child to bed myself, Berta,' he said. 'You go and get some sleep. You have been very brave.' Then he gave her first his hand, and second a twenty-mark note.

'Thank you very much,' said fat Berta. 'You know something? So long as we get advance notice, I don't mind burglars at all.' Then she too went to her own room.

Mr Pogge helped Dot to get undressed and washed. Then she lay down, and Piefke got into bed with her. Her father sat on the side of the bed. 'Luise,' he said seriously, 'listen to me, my child.' She took his large hand in her small hands and looked into his eyes.

'You know that I love you very much, don't you?' he asked quietly. 'But I can't spend a lot of time looking after you, because I have to earn money. Why do you do such things? Why do you lie to us? I'll never be easy in my mind if I know that I can't trust you.'

Dot stroked his hand. 'Yes, I know you don't have much time because you have to earn money,' she said. 'But Mama doesn't have to earn money, and all the same she doesn't have time for me. You don't either of you have time for me. Now I'll be having another governess, and we can't tell in advance what will come of that.'

'I know,' he said. 'You're quite right. But will you promise always to tell the truth in future? That would reassure me a great deal.'

Dot smiled at him. 'All right, if it reassures you a great deal.'

He kissed her goodnight. When he turned at the door to switch off the light she said, 'But all the same, Director, it was very interesting.'

In spite of all the tablets he swallowed, Mr Pogge had a sleepless night.

ABOUT GRATITUDE

Fat Berta was brave, don't you think? Hitting burglars over the head wasn't supposed to be part of her job, but she did it all the same. That kind of thing deserves gratitude. But what does Mrs Pogge do? She goes to bed and falls asleep!

However, Mr Pogge gives Berta first his hand and second a twenty-mark note. Many such gentlemen might only give her his hand, although he has plenty of money. Others might only give her the twenty marks, although he has a hand to shake hers. Mr Pogge has both and gives her both. First he shakes fat Berta's hand, then he gives her money. I think he did it in the right order. After all, he could have given her the banknote first, and then he could have shaken her hand, saying, 'And by the way, thank you too.'

No, he does it all just as he should. He acts exactly right.

The more I get to know Mr Pogge, the better I like him. In fact he seems to me nicer from chapter to chapter. And the same can be said of the last chapter, which comes next.

Chapter Sixteen

All's Well that Ends Well

When Dot came out of school the next day, for a change her father's car was standing outside the school gate. And this time her father was actually in it, as well as Mr Hollack. He waved to her. The other little girls were furious. Once again, there wasn't any prospect of a drive in the car!

Dot said hello to the chauffeur, and got in. 'Is anything wrong?' she asked anxiously.

'No,' said her father. 'I just happen to have some time today.'

'You have some what?' she asked, looking at him as if he had suddenly sprouted a bushy beard. 'Time?'

Mr Pogge felt really embarrassed in front of his small daughter. 'Well, yes,' he said. 'Don't ask such silly questions. I suppose a man can have time to spare now and then.'

'That's great,' she cried. 'Shall we go to Charlottenhof Palace and eat cream puffs?' Charlottenhof Palace is in a lovely park near Berlin.

'I thought it would be a better idea to pick up your friend Anton from school.'

Then she hugged her father and gave him a kiss that sounded like cannon fire. They drove off to Anton's school and arrived just in time. Anton almost fell over backwards when he saw the beautiful car waiting for him, with Dot and her father in it. Dot waved to him to go over to them, and her father shook hands with him and told him he was a splendid fellow. He had fixed things brilliantly to outwit Robert the Devil, said Mr Pogge.

'It was the obvious thing to do, sir,' said Anton. Then he was invited to sit beside Mr Hollack, who sometimes let him step on the accelerator and work the indicators. It was wonderful.

Dot pulled at her father's ear and whispered, 'Director, Anton can even cook.'

'Is there anything he can't do?' asked Mr Pogge.

'Anton? Anton can do anything,' she said proudly. And since Anton could do anything, they drove to Charlottenhof Palace after all and ate cream puffs. Even Mr Pogge ate one, although the doctor had strictly forbidden him to eat cream puffs. Then they all three played hide and seek so that Dot's father would lose weight, because he was getting a paunch. After that Anton wanted to go home, but the director said he would tell Anton's mother all about it.

'Has Mr Bremser been cross with you again?' asked Dot.

'No,' said Anton. 'He's been really nice to me recently, and he's invited me to have coffee with him.'

'There you are, then,' said Dot calmly. But she was so pleased that she pinched her calves under the table.

They got back very late for lunch. Mrs Pogge felt deeply injured, but the other three were so happy that they didn't even notice. So Mrs Pogge felt even more injured, and she couldn't eat anything at all or she would have burst.

'I wonder where Miss Andacht is?' asked Anton, because he had a good heart. Mrs Pogge didn't understand such feelings. She only murmured, 'Where in the world are we going to find a reliable governess now?'

Mr Pogge had a sudden inspiration. He took Dot aside, whispered to her and then said, 'I'll be right back.' Then he disappeared.

The others ate without talking much. After lunch, the two children went to Dot's room, where Piefke was eagerly waiting for them.

Anton had to sit on a chair while the others acted the story of Little Red Riding Hood for him. Piefke knew his part very well by now, but he still didn't want to eat Dot up. 'Maybe he'll learn how when he's a couple of years older,' she said. Anton thought it had been an excellent performance all the same, and clapped as if he were in a theatre. Dot took a bow ten times and blew kisses, and Piefke barked until he got a sugar lump.

'What shall we play next?' asked Dot. 'I could do *The Hunchbacked Tailor and his Son*. Or we could play mother and child, with Piefke as the baby? No, let's play burglars! You be

Robert the Devil, I'll be fat Berta, and when you come through the door I'll hit you over the head with the club.'

'And who's going to play the three policemen?' he asked.

'I'll be Berta and the three policemen,' said Dot.

'You can't dance with yourself,' Anton objected. So that was no good either. 'I know what,' he said. 'We'll play the discovery of America and I'll be Columbus.'

'Good,' cried Dot. 'I'll be America and Piefke is the egg.'

'The what?'

'He's the egg,' she said. 'Columbus's egg.' But Anton didn't know about that; he hadn't reached it yet at his school.

'Here's another idea,' he said. 'We can play crossing the ocean in a folding boat.' They cleared the table and turned it upside down so that its legs were sticking up in the air. That was the boat. And while Anton was making the tablecloth into a sail, Dot went to the larder to fetch ship's provisions: a pot of jam, the butter dish, several knives and forks, two pounds of potatoes, a dish of pear compote and half a salami sausage. 'Salami is a good idea,' she said. 'It keeps for months.' So they packed the provisions into the boat, and then there was just room for the children and the dog. They put a bowl of water beside the table. Dot splashed about in it from time to time as they sailed over the ocean, and said, 'The sea is terribly cold.' In the middle of the ocean Anton got out, fetched some salt and sprinkled it into the bowl. He said that seawater had to be salty.

Then there was a dead calm. It lasted for three weeks. Anton rowed with walking sticks, but they hardly moved from the spot. Dot and he and Piefke ate the salami, and Dot wailed, 'Cap'n, we've nearly finished the provisions.'

'We must hold out,' said Anton. 'I see Rio de Janeiro over there.' And he pointed to the bed.

'Thank God,' said Dot. 'Otherwise I'd have starved to death.' Although in fact she was so full, what with lunch and the salami sausage, that she felt quite queasy.

'Here comes a terrible storm,' said Anton. He got out and rocked the table. 'Help!' shouted Dot in despair. 'We're sinking!' Then she threw the two pounds of potatoes overboard to lighten the cargo. But Anton and the storm kept raging. Dot clutched her tummy and said, 'I feel seasick.' And because waves as high as houses were breaking over them, Piefke fell into the bowl, along with the pear compote, sending water splashing up.

At last the storm died down, the boy pushed the table over to the bed, and they came ashore in Rio de Janeiro. The local population gave the mariners a hearty welcome, and all three of them were photographed. Piefke had curled up and was enthusiastically licking his sticky coat. It tasted of pear sauce.

'Thank you for your friendly reception,' said Dot. 'We have endured a voyage of great deprivations, but we will look back on it happily. I'm afraid my dress is done for, so I'm going home on the railway. Better safe than sorry.'

'I am Antonio Gastiglione, Lord Mayor of Rio de Janeiro,' said the boy. 'I welcome you to our city, and I name you and your dog world champions at ocean crossing.'

'Thank you, kind sir,' said Dot. 'We will always treasure your cup.' So saying, she picked up the butter dish and said, with the air of an expert, 'Genuine silver, at least ten thousand carats.'

Then the door opened and Anton's mother came in. That was a very happy moment. 'Mr Pogge fetched me in his car,' she said. 'But my goodness, what do you think it looks like in here?'

'We've just been crossing the ocean,' Dot told her, and then they tidied up the room. Piefke wanted to get into the water and pear compote again of his own accord, but Anton's mother wouldn't let him.

Meanwhile, Mr Pogge had a serious conversation with his wife. 'I want Dot to grow up to be a good sort of girl,' he said. 'I can do without another Miss Andacht in this place. I'm not having my child turn into a stuck-up goose. She must learn that life is serious. Dot has chosen her own friends, and I approve of her choice. If you looked after the child more, that would be different, but now I've made my decision. Not a word against it, please! I've said yes to whatever you wanted long enough. It's going to be different from now on.'

Mrs Pogge had tears in her eyes. 'Yes, Fritz, whatever you say,' she said, mopping her face with her handkerchief. 'That's fine, but you mustn't be cross with me any more.' He gave her a kiss, and then he asked Anton's mother to come into the room and asked what she thought about his plan. Mrs Gast was touched, and said that if his wife was happy about it she would gladly agree. She was very happy herself.

'Now, pay attention, children!' said Mr Pogge. 'Listen to me. Anton's mother is moving into Miss Andacht's old room today. We'll get the bedroom with the green wallpaper ready for Anton, and from now on we'll all live together. All right?'

Anton couldn't say a word. He shook hands with Mr Pogge and his wife. Then he hugged his mother and whispered, 'We won't have so much to worry about now, will we?'

'No, my dear boy,' she said.

Then Anton sat down beside Dot again, and she was so pleased that she pulled his ears. Piefke trotted comfortably round the room. It looked as if he were smiling.

'Well, is that all right, dear daughter?' asked Dot's father, stroking her hair. 'And in the long summer holidays we'll go to the Baltic Sea with Mrs Gast and Anton.'

Then Dot went out of the room, and when she came back she was carrying a box of cigars in one hand and matches in the other. 'As a reward,' she said. Her father lit a cigar, gave a little grunt of pleasure as the first cloud of smoke rose, and said, 'I've earned this.'

THE SIXTEENTH AFTERTHOUGHT IS:

ABOUT A HAPPY ENDING

So now we have come to the end of this book, and it is a proper happy ending. All the characters have arrived in the places that are right for them, and we can leave them to live out the rest of their stories, trusting to the future. Miss Andacht's fiancé is in prison, Anton and his mother are in luck, Dot is happy in the company of her friend Anton and Miss Andacht is in the soup. They are all where they ought to be. Fate has made a story to measure.

Now that might lead you to think that life always works out fairly and comes to a happy ending, like the story in this book. But if you do, you would be making a bad mistake. It ought to be like that, and all sensible people try hard to make it turn out as it should. However, it doesn't. Not yet.

I was once at school with a boy who regularly copied from his neighbour in class. Do you think he was punished for it? No, it was the neighbour he copied from who got punished. Don't be too surprised if life punishes you sometime for what wasn't your fault. When you grow up, make sure that things turn out better! We haven't quite managed it yet. Try to be better, more honest, fairer and more sensible than most of us grown-ups have been!

They say that the earth was a paradise once upon a time. Anything is possible.

The earth could be a paradise again one day. Everything is possible.

A Little Postscript

*A*lthough *the story of Dot, Anton and Piefke is over now, I still have something on my mind.*

It's this: children who know my other book, Emil and the Detectives, *could say, 'Dear Mr Kästner, your Anton is a boy just like your Emil. Why didn't you write about a boy who was entirely different in your new book?'*

And as that is not an entirely unjustified question, I would like to tell you the answer before I put the last full stop to this story. I wrote about Anton, although he really is like Emil Tischbein, because I believe that we can't tell too many stories about boys like that, and we can't have too many Emils and Antons.

Perhaps you will decide to be like them? Perhaps, if you have come to like them and think they are good examples, you will be as hard-working, right-minded, brave and honourable as they are?

That would be the best reward I could have. Because Emil, Anton and all who are like them will grow up to be very good men. The kind of men we can always do with.

ERICH KÄSTNER, writer, poet and journalist, was born in Dresden in 1899. His first children's book, *Emil and the Detectives*, was published in 1929 and has since been translated into nearly 60 languages and sold millions of copies all over the world. After the Nazis took power in Germany, Kästner's books were burnt and he was excluded from the writers' guild. He won many awards, including the prestigious Hans Christian Andersen Award in 1960. He died in 1974.

WALTER TRIER was an acclaimed cartoonist and illustrator, and Kästner's collaborator on more than a dozen children's books.

ANTHEA BELL is an illustrious, award-winning translator, best known for her translations of the much-loved Asterix books and the work of Zweig and Sebald.

PUSHKIN CHILDREN'S BOOKS

Just as we all are, children are fascinated by stories. From the earliest age, we love to hear about monsters and heroes, romance and death, disaster and rescue, from every place and time.

We created Pushkin Children's Books to share these tales from different languages and cultures with younger readers, and to open the door to the wide, colourful worlds these stories offer.

From picture books and adventure stories to fairy tales and classics, and from fifty-year-old bestsellers to current huge successes abroad, the books on the Pushkin Children's list reflect the very best stories from around the world, for our most discerning readers of all: children.

THE WITCH IN THE BROOM CUPBOARD
AND OTHER TALES
PIERRE GRIPARI

Illustrated by Fernando Puig Rosado

'Wonderful... funny, tender and daft'
David Almond

THE STORY OF THE BLUE PLANET
ANDRI SNÆR MAGNASON

Illustrated by Áslaug Jónsdóttir

'A Seussian mix of wonder, wit and gravitas'
The New York Times

SHOLA AND THE LIONS
BERNARDO ATXAGA

Illustrated by Mikel Valverde

'Gently ironic stories... totally charming'
Independent

THE POINTLESS LEOPARD:
WHAT GOOD ARE KIDS ANYWAY?
COLAS GUTMAN

Illustrated by Delphine Perret

'Lively, idiomatic and always entertaining...
a decidedly offbeat little book'
Robert Dunbar, *Irish Times*

POCKETY: THE TORTOISE WHO LIVED AS SHE PLEASED

FLORENCE SEYVOS

Illustrated by Claude Ponti

'A treasure – a real find – and one of the most enjoyable children's books I've read in a while... This is a tortoise that deserves to win every literary race'
Observer

THE LETTER FOR THE KING

TONKE DRAGT

'Gripping from its opening moment onwards, this award-winning book doesn't miss a beat from its thrilling beginning to its satisfying ending'
Julia Eccleshare

THE PILOT AND THE LITTLE PRINCE

PETER SÍS

'With its extraordinary, sophisticated illustrations, its poetry and the historical detail of the text, this book will reward readers of any age over eight'
Sunday Times

SAVE THE STORY

GULLIVER · ANTIGONE · CAPTAIN NEMO · DON JUAN
GILGAMESH · THE BETROTHED · THE NOSE
CYRANO DE BERGERAC · KING LEAR · CRIME AND PUNISHMENT

'An amazing new series from Pushkin Press in which literary, adult authors retell classics (with terrific illustrations) for a younger generation'
Daily Telegraph

THE CAT WHO CAME IN OFF THE ROOF

ANNIE M.G. SCHMIDT

'Guaranteed to make anyone 7-plus to 107 who likes to
curl up with a book and a cat purr with pleasure'
The Times

THE OKSA POLLOCK SERIES

ANNE PLICHOTA AND CENDRINE WOLF

Part 1 · *The Last Hope*

Part 2 · *The Forest of Lost Souls*

Part 3 · *The Heart of Two Worlds*

'A feisty heroine, lots of sparky tricks and evil opponents
could fill a gap left by the end of the Harry Potter series'
Daily Mail

THE VITELLO SERIES

KIM FUPZ AAKESON

Illustrated by Niels Bo Bojesen

'Full of quirky humour and an anarchic sense
of fun that children will love'
Booktrust

A HOUSE WITHOUT MIRRORS

MÅRTEN SANDÉN

Illustrated by Moa Schulman

'A classic story that has it all'
Dagens Nyheter